BECAUSE *of* GRÁCIA

TOM SIMES

DEXTERITY

NASHVILLE

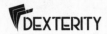

Dexterity LLC 604 Magnolia Lane, Nashville, TN 37211

The author gratefully acknowledges the photography of Nick Arnold and Five Stones Films for allowing the use of images in this book. All rights reserved to Nick Arnold/Five Stones Films.

First edition: 2017 10 9 8 7 6 5 4 3 2 1
Printed in the United States of America.

Library of Congress Cataloging-in-Publication Data
Authors: Tom Simes

ISBN: 978-1-947297-00-5 (Paperback) 978-1-947297-01-2 (eBook)

Book design by Brian Kannard with Sarah Siegand
Cover design by Trent Design Inc.

To my wife, Michelle, and our four kids, Brett, Brooklyn, Bree, and Brolin: Thank you for inspiring me, encouraging me, and supporting all of my artistic endeavors.

You've truly been the wind in my sails.

ONE
SENIOR YEAR

It was Chase's senior year when he first met Grace.

The day started like every first day of school he'd ever known: His eyes popped open when his alarm went off at 5:25 a.m. He blinked a few times, realizing he'd hardly slept. He stretched, yawned, then heard a few loud knocks, followed by "Everybody Plays the Fool," from other side of the door.

It was his dad—singing, if you could call it that. Chase had once compared it to the sound of an animal fighting to get out of a trap. When he did, though, his dad started singing at the top of his lungs and broke into song again every time he saw him for the next few days. Chase promised himself he'd never say anything about it again.

Chase stared at the ceiling. His dad burst into the room, using a wooden spoon as a microphone. His dad loved '70s tunes and quizzed him on them whenever they could find an oldies station in the car. To his dad, the early '70s was "the golden age of melody." Whenever Chase heard a song now, his mind automatically ran through the title, artist, and year. *"Everybody Plays the Fool," the Main Ingredient, 1972*, he thought. Followed by, *Time to get up, first day of school, wanna be early.*

Then, *Senior year.*

Chase sat up and gave a cat-like yawn. He arched his back, stretching to wake up.

His dad hit the high note as if he were trying to shatter glass.

Dropping his feet to the floor, Chase took the edge of his pillow in his right hand, then flung it across the room as hard as he could at his dad. There was a solid, satisfying *Whump!*

"Ah, good, you're awake," his dad said, the pillow now in his right hand. Chase wasn't sure how his dad was still standing. "Breakfast in half an hour. See you there!"

Chase knew what was coming next. He ducked, and the pillow hit his headboard, hard.

* * * * *

"Grá-ci-a . . .

"Grá-ci-a . . . it's time."

Grácia's mother lay on her bed behind her, rubbing her daughter's arm. Her mother's breath tickled her ear. Grácia smiled. As her eyes opened she was caught off guard again by waking up in an unfamiliar place. *Oh, right*, she thought. *New room. New town. New school.*

Again.

She took a deep breath. The air seemed heavy. *Humidity,* she remembered. *Right. Not California—Louisiana.*

"Time for school, Grácia."

New school, she thought again. *New town.*

Senior year.

* * * * *

As Chase got ready, he couldn't believe he'd graduate in just a matter of months. He couldn't believe he was almost eighteen. He couldn't believe he was supposed to go to college next year. It was all coming so fast.

All he'd known his whole life was working in the family hardware store, going to school, going to church, and hanging out with his best friend, OB. All he'd known was living this life, in this house, in the same place: Baton Rouge. It was just beginning to dawn on him that there might be something beyond all of this—the only problem was he had no idea what.

His parents told him they named him Chase because they had high hopes he'd go after something—that he'd be a man of action—that he'd do something great with his life—to, as Steve Jobs once put it, "Put a dent in the universe." Instead, he realized, he'd done the opposite. He avoided conflict at all costs. He never spoke up. One time when OB was giving him a hard time about being such a wallflower, he told Chase that if he were a superhero, they'd call him "Undercover Man." Chase had laughed at the time, but he was no longer sure he thought it was funny.

After taking a shower, brushing his teeth, putting on deodorant, and doing his usual set of Mr. Universe poses in the mirror, Chase got dressed and went down for breakfast.

* * * * *

"Did you sleep well, Chase?" his mom asked.

Chase picked at his pancakes, listening to music on his iPhone through his headphones—headphones he never went anywhere without. His little sister, Olivia, sat twirling eggs on the end of her fork. When she saw he wasn't listening, she tugged at his sleeve and nodded toward their mom.

Chase took off his headphones. "Huh?"

"You sleep okay?"

"Fine." There was an edge to his voice.

"You nervous?" his dad asked.

"Mm-mm." Chase shrugged.

His mom and dad exchanged concerned-parent looks.

"OB gonna meet you there early?" his mom asked, probing now.

Chase laughed. "Seriously, Mom?" Chase imagined OB nose-down in his pillow with his rear end stuck in the air like a teepee. No way he was up yet.

Chase took another bite of pancake and realized he wasn't hungry. He looked at his iPhone for the time. "Better, ah, go, actually. Bye, Mom—Pop. See ya, Olivia."

His dad looked at the wall clock. "That's my boy!" He smiled. He grabbed an imaginary jacket lapel and emphasized each word with his index finger. "Early bird gets the worm!"

Olivia waved, having finally put the forkful of scrambled eggs into her mouth.

Chase got up from the table, took his longboard and backpack, and headed for the door.

Every year, until last year, his dad had grabbed him just before he could get away, calling out, "Morgan sandwich!" His mom and dad squeezed him between them and his sister would fit in wherever she could with both arms around him. Then they would pray. He cringed slightly at the memory. Finally, last year, he told his dad he was old enough to pray for himself. He was almost eighteen, after all. The memory came back vividly in his mind. As he sauntered down the hallway to the front door, he began daydreaming about last year at this time. He shook his head as if trying to clear away the image.

Chase could feel his dad smiling in the doorway of their house as he skated to the corner of the block. He didn't look back, but as he turned toward the school, a smile spread over his face as well. His parents might drive him a little crazy now and again, but he loved them for it all the same. He couldn't help it.

He pulled his headphones back up to his ears, selected a playlist on his iPhone, and skated down the street toward his senior year.

* * * * *

John C. Livingston unlocked the door to his room at 6:00 a.m. sharp. The school was quiet and empty, except for the janitor who usually got in around the same time. Though many of the teachers arrived with the students, rushed around all day, then stayed late grading papers or tests, John Livingston got his work done before school and left promptly at 4:00 p.m. for either rugby practice or a workout. He had a reputation for never taking work home.

John Livingston did things differently.

He crossed to his desk and began getting ready for the day. Each day, as part of his ritual, he rearranged the things on his desk. He organized the assignments for each period into special folders along the left side, tidied up whatever else seemed out of place, then finished by lining up four pencils—freshly sharpened—across the front center of his desk. He had a coffee cup that held only green pens—he didn't use red for correcting—in the right-hand corner. Once everything was the way he liked it on his desk, he worked around the exterior of the room, sorting and organizing books on their shelves, checking for dust, writing his quote of the day on his chalkboard, and whatever else he felt needed his attention.

Then, lastly, before sitting at his desk and either marking assignments or going over his lesson plans one more time, he double-checked the alignment of the desks in the room meticulously, arranging them into five rows of six chairs each.

He aligned each outside row with the edges of the chalkboards and evenly sorted each chair into its own little island of space.

Since it was the first day of school and he knew his first day routine and lectures by heart, he headed to the teacher's room for a cup of coffee. He'd be back in his room at least five minutes before the first bell rang.

* * * * *

"Where's the common sense?" Grácia's father blurted out. He was staring hard at the paper in one hand, his coffee cup poised halfway to his mouth in the other. "Gracie, finish this statement for me: 'If you create grasslands, it increases overall land area, thereby absorbing more heat during the day and . . .'"

Grácia looked up from her Bible. "Radiating it at night."

"Bingo!" he exclaimed, hardly looking up from the paper to smile.

Grácia smiled back.

Her mom looked up at each of them over the top of her open laptop. Grácia's brother, Jonah, sat unrolling his cinnamon roll into a long snake and making it crawl across his plate.

Grácia dropped her eyes back to her Bible, avoiding her mother's look of concern.

Grácia's mom whispered to her husband, hoping Grácia wouldn't hear. "Did we make the right decision?"

"No!" Dr. Davis blurted. "This is too complex to simplify into a talking point!"

Closing her laptop, Mrs. Davis gave her husband the look. "Andrew!"

Grácia smiled and shook her head.

Her dad set the paper down and took off his glasses. "Sorry, hon, did you ask me something?"

"It's her senior year. Shouldn't we have stayed in California?"

Her dad raised his eyebrows. "No, honey. We all agreed this was the right move. Gracie's resilient. She'll be fine."

Grácia's iPhone chirped softly. She picked it up—another text from Michael. *What is it, like four-something a.m. in California?* She deleted the message without reading it and put her phone in a side pocket of her backpack. "Dad, I'm ready to go. Mom, Jonah's just playing." She hoped that would distract her mom from worrying about California any more.

Her mother looked at Jonah and her face darkened. "Hey! *Eat!*"

Jonah picked up his cinnamon roll snake and put the head of it into his open mouth without biting down. "Ahhhh."

His mom pointed at him. "Stop now or I will beat you!" she cried, emphasizing each word as she gave him her meanest look. Jonah smiled, knowing his mom didn't mean it, that her bark was always worse than her bite. She glanced over at Grácia. "Bye, sweetie! I love you!"

"I love you too, Momma!" Grácia yelled back as she headed for the garage.

* * * * *

Sylvester, the school custodian, had just drawn the flag to the top of the pole when Chase rounded the corner to Eastglenn High. Sylvester was an old-school patriot who teared up every morning as he saluted the stars and stripes. Chase smiled and waved as he skated by, and Sylvester waved back. Chase was one of the few that gave him the time of day, so he always made sure to acknowledge him.

Since being late to the first day of kindergarten with OB, Chase had made it a policy to always be earlier than everyone else on the first day of school. Over the years, he'd come earlier and earlier. By high school, he was probably way too early, but he was always up at the crack of dawn to go to work with his dad during the summer—so it just sort of happened. All the same, he liked having the school all to himself, even if just for a little while. That gave him time to find his locker, put his things away, get whatever he needed for his first class, then take some time to chill, listen to music, and wander off into his thoughts.

* * * * *

A warm grin spread across Zach Brady's face as he unlocked the door to his classroom. He was greeted by the musty wood smell he'd grown familiar with over the last few years. To most, it would have seemed an ordinary classroom with pale green walls—not incredibly well or imaginatively decorated—but for Zach Brady each element had meaning, right down to the General John Stark bobblehead whose base read "Live Free or Die." One of his first classes had gotten him that. Then there was the replica of an original map of the thirteen colonies used by President Washington on the west wall. He'd picked that up from the gift shop while visiting the Mount Vernon estate on his honeymoon. The window ledge to the east was home to a miniature set of Civil War cannons from a trip to Gettysburg. The rest of the room had little mementos all over, from the poster of Gast's *American Progress* he got at the Smithsonian to the World War I poster of Uncle Sam that read "I Want You." Across the back wall of the classroom was a homemade banner that read: "Beware of myth becoming legend and legend becoming history!"

He crossed behind his desk and surveyed the room. Everything seemed to be in place. Then he pulled out his chair, slid his bag under his desk, and turned to the whiteboard behind him. In barely legible letters, he wrote, "Mr. Brady." Then, below that, "Seize the day"—underlining it for emphasis. He always smiled at his poor penmanship, but the kids liked the fact that his handwriting looked more like theirs than Mr. Livingston's impeccable calligraphy.

Turning back to his desk, he sat down, something he almost never did during class. Everything seemed to be in place. Then, as was his normal routine, he opened a drawer and pulled out his Bible. He liked to read a verse or two from Proverbs every morning to center him before things got crazy.

Zach looked at his watch: sixteen minutes until the first bell. He knew a small trickle of students would be wandering into his room soon. He was well liked and kids often dropped in just to say hi and shoot the breeze with him. He got up from his desk and sat down in one of the front-row desks, then quietly folded his hands to pray for the year ahead.

* * * * *

The Davises' SUV stopped in the street in front of the school with a line of other cars that were starting to trickle in. Clusters of students were congregating in front of the school as others wandered inside. Grácia climbed out of the SUV and started across the lawn.

Dr. Davis rolled down the passenger window and yelled after her, "Knock 'em dead, Gracie!"

Clutching her books to her chest with both hands, Grácia smiled again but didn't turn around. She dropped her right hand to her side and gave him an underhand wave, skipped a few steps, and headed into the school. Dr. Davis nodded to himself, smiled, then drove away.

From the back recesses of her mind, a thought came to Grácia: *Where did I put my schedule?*

TWO
LIVINGSTON'S CLASS

Chase stood before the large auditorium. Feet stomped rhythmically, interspersed with a synchronized clap.

Thump, thump, clap! Thump, thumb, clap!

With a microphone in one hand, he took center stage and lowered his head. The lights dimmed. The rhythm quieted, expectantly. A steady beat on a snare drum began behind him. He began to chant with the beat of the drum,

"He didn't fight to settle the score,
He fought for the poor
and went to the parts of the city that
the rich wouldn't even dare think about—"

"*Guv'nah!* We're late for Livingston's class. He's gonna have our glorious glutes for breakfast!"

OB shook Chase, but it didn't seem to have any effect. He reached down and slapped Chase's headphones off his head. Chase's eyes sprang open and he looked up at OB as if he had just doused him with a bucket of ice water. He was back at school daydreaming—again. *Did I actually fall asleep this time?* He closed the notebook in his lap where he'd been writing spoken-word lyrics and looked at his phone—about a minute to get to class. OB pulled him to his feet and pushed him on ahead.

OB had called Chase "Guv'nah" for as long as he could remember. It started after OB watched *Mary Poppins* like twenty times. Chase was uncomfortable with it at first, since the name inferred he was a leader or something, and that was definitely not his thing. But it grew on him. Besides, he liked having a nickname.

Since OB had given him a nickname, he felt obligated to do the same—so he started calling his best friend "OB-Wan." It made sense. OB was his only friend, too, and what could be better than being named after a Jedi Master?

"You're here forty-five minutes before anyone else and you can't get to class on time. What's wrong with you?"

It seemed like yesterday Chase and OB were running late to kindergarten. "Shortcut, Guv-nah?" OB had exclaimed. "Why do I listen to you? We're late—again!"

"Sorry OB-Wan, but I found something really cool to show the class." Chase had pulled the snake from under his jacket as they ran into the classroom, where they were greeted by a chorus of shrieks.

Some things never change, Chase thought.

As they made their way through the halls, Chase noticed Bobbi Ryan leaning against her locker with Jesse Valentine standing over her, their faces almost nose to nose. Chase had known Bobbi for years. He'd gone to church with her as long as he could remember, and Bobbi's dad was the pastor. Chase had always thought she was pretty, and he'd had a thing for her in junior high but never told her. He knew Jesse by reputation only. Something felt wrong about seeing Jesse with Bobbi, but Chase didn't have time to think about it. He didn't want to be late to Livingston's class on the very first day.

* * * * *

At the lockers, Bobbi stared into Jesse's eyes. She'd had him pretty much all to herself over the summer, but now he seemed distracted again, like when they went to the mall together. He was only half-listening. His head always spun around like he was looking for something, but she could never figure out what. All she knew was that it wasn't her. Though she couldn't really put her finger on it, they just seemed closer when she had him all to herself.

She looked at the nearest clock as Chase Morgan and OB Zachariah raced past them. Jesse's head turned to look, then lingered a bit longer when two girls came from the other direction in their short uniform skirts. One of them smiled.

"I gotta go," he said.

"Walk me to class," Bobbi pleaded, knowing he was going to follow the girls.

"Bobbi! You're gonna make me late for debate! You know what Livingston's like!"

She placed her hands on the sides of his face and gently turned it back toward her. "Please!" Not thinking, she pulled him closer to whisper in his ear, "My parents are gone tonight." Then she gave him a kiss.

He gave her the big, goofy grin she loved so much. She melted a little.

"Okay," he said, "but I've really gotta run."

* * * * *

As the second bell rang, Chase and OB ran through the doorway.

"Gentlemen!" Mr. Livingston's voice boomed. He had a reputation for being the toughest teacher in the school when it came to tardiness.

Chase and OB stopped dead in their tracks as Chase slid into the back of OB, pushing him precariously close to Livingston.

Mr. Livingston took a breath and pursed his lips. Through almost gritted teeth, he said, "Find a seat."

OB turned and raised his eyebrows, then darted to the closest open desk. Chase looked over the classroom and saw a couple of empty seats near the back row and circled around to the one furthest back. In the process, he noticed Amy Daniels sitting in one of the desks in the second row. Amy used to go to youth group with Bobbi, OB, and him. He remembered that if there was a "like" on one of his Instagram photos from camp, it was usually from Amy. All the same, he hadn't seen her in church all summer. Maybe it had been even longer than that, he realized. He tried to shoot her a smile, but she avoided making eye contact as he hustled to his seat.

Mr. Livingston addressed the room in a commanding voice. "Ladies and gentlemen, please stand with me."

Everyone stood and put their hands over their hearts. Together they recited, "I pledge allegiance to the flag of the United States of America, and to the republic for which it stands, one nation under God, indivisible, with liberty and justice for all."

Though most classes didn't recite the pledge anymore, it was one of the things that John C. Livingston was famous for. That and his Kiwi accent, as well as his reputation as one of the toughest and most sought-after teachers at Eastglenn. He'd come over from New Zealand on a teacher exchange program fifteen years before and liked it so well that he stayed. It took him seven years to become a naturalized US citizen, and like a lot of naturalized citizens, he seemed to take all things American more seriously than those born into it.

The US seemed to love him back as well. He'd won the state Teacher of the Year award four times at Eastglenn, and his speech and advanced debate classes were always full. At one point Principal Schaub had tried to close advanced debate to anyone who didn't have a GPA of 3.25 or higher, but Livingston had fought the restriction. He and Principal Schaub had gone toe to toe over it, and Schaub was no lightweight. He'd spent his entire career at Eastglenn and in that time had turned it into one of the most prestigious schools in the state.

The issue went all the way to the school board, with parents fighting on both sides. In the largest gathering to ever attend a school board meeting, arguments were presented and Mr. Livingston made an impassioned plea for equality that would have made the founding fathers proud. Keeping the class open to all GPAs won by a single board member's vote. It seemed Schaub was never going to get over having Livingston best him. To placate the losers, the school board asked that the class only be available to seniors. Livingston agreed to the terms but put Principal Schaub on notice that he wasn't afraid to stand up to him—something the rest of the staff was afraid to do.

Mr. Livingston's room wasn't like other classrooms either. The ceiling was twice as high and the room was twice as long as a regular classroom. It used to be the choral room but Livingston convinced the choral teacher to move down the hall into another room when he was in his fifth year at Eastglenn. Since then, he had made this room his home. The room even smelled different, smelled . . . important. When you walked in you felt as if you were entering a college lecture hall.

A line of pictures ran across the front above the movable chalkboard. They looked down like a gallery of jurors. From left to right ran the faces of Friedrich Nietzsche, Karl Marx, George Carlin, Vincent van Gogh, Bruce Lee, Charles Darwin, Jay Gould, Albert Einstein, Henry Fonda, Charlie Chaplin, and Mark Twain. Dead center, dividing Bruce Lee and Darwin, hung the American flag, which was right behind the lectern from which students addressed the class during debates.

After everyone was seated again, Mr. Livingston took the lectern in both hands and addressed the class. "Welcome to Debate 30. This is a comprehensive course that will challenge you to think for yourself. In here, dialectic reasoning is your friend—"

There was a knock at the door. Ms. Stevens walked in, and Mr. Livingston brightened considerably. Ms. Stevens, one of the school counselors, was pretty, played the guitar, and sang at coffee shops around town every once in a while. There were rumors that Mr. Livingston never missed a show. Josie Fullerton and Zabrina Du Bois exchanged looks that were somewhere between acknowledging a shared secret and complete disdain.

A new girl followed Ms. Stevens in. Most of the guys sat up a little straighter and looked at each other, nodding their approval. Josie noticed the boys' reaction immediately and looked over at Zabrina with a look that clearly communicated, *Competition.*

"So sorry for the interruption, Mr. Livingston."

"No problem, Ms. Stevens. What can I do for you?"

"We have a new student from California who had a little trouble finding your class this morning. I had to get her a new copy of her schedule." She handed it to Mr. Livingston.

He took it, smiling broadly at Ms. Stevens. He looked at it, then turned to the class. "Class, I'd like to introduce you to Grácia Davis." He impressed Grácia with the way he pronounced her name, as most people usually had a hard time saying it properly. *"Eso es español para la Grácia, sí?"*

"Sí. Habla español?"

"No, hablo muy poco español—and very poorly, *very* poorly," Mr. Livingston responded. He looked at her puzzled. *"España?"*

"Mi madre es de Puerto Rico."

"Ah, sí." Mr. Livingston nodded, even though all he had understood was "Puerto Rico."

Two of the guys on the other side of Chase, Jorge Harder and Cisco Diaz, shook their heads in astonishment. "The guy even knows how to speak Spanish. What doesn't he know?" Cisco whispered. Livingston swung around and gave him a look that said, *Quiet down.*

"Please, Grácia, take a seat." Livingston smiled as he pointed to the open seat in front of Chase. He then turned and said, "Thank you, Ms. Stevens," with a noticeably pleasant tone. Josie coyly smiled at Zabrina and Amy. Last spring Josie had started a rumor that Livingston and Ms. Stevens had something for each other, and this latest encounter only backed her up.

Grácia smiled, nodding shyly. As she crossed by OB he turned his head toward Chase and mouthed, "Wow!"

Chase's eyes grew as big as saucers.

Eastglenn already had a reputation for pretty girls. In the last decade, the four closest high schools had fallen to squabbling over when to hold their proms since a lot of the jocks and rich seniors from other schools would boycott theirs if it were on the same night as Eastglenn's. They'd be going to Eastglenn's, after all, with one of the prettiest girls in town.

To top it all, Josie Fullerton had supposedly set some kind of unofficial record by getting taken to the prom at four local high schools the year before—and it was rumored that she'd ditched her date at Robert E. Lee to go to a fraternity party at LSU with Lee's star pitcher from the season before. He "just happened" to drop by their prom that night, and soon after that, Josie was nowhere to be found.

To Chase, however, this new girl was something beyond all of that. He couldn't take his eyes off of her.

With black hair and bright eyes the color of milk chocolate, Grácia walked confidently past the "popular" girls. Josie glared and Amy popped her bubble gum, but Grácia ignored them, which only made them angrier. She'd seen girls like this before and knew acknowledging them would only empower them.

For Chase, the whole room was in slow motion. He didn't realize he was staring until Grácia turned down his row and looked right at him. It was as if she looked right into his soul. And that smile again. He stiffened slightly, nodded, and realized he was staring. Trying to play it cool, he started looking for his notebook in his backpack, even though it was out on his desk.

Mr. Livingston was back at the lectern, and the room grew still again. "Why do we debate?"

OB raised his hand, and Mr. Livingston nodded to him. "To find the truth."

"Precisely," Livingston agreed. "I hope you're all thankful for the beginning of another year—"

There was another knock at the door. Mr. Livingston looked at the clock, perturbed. He could see Jesse Valentine's face through the small window in the door.

When Mr. Livingston opened the door for him, Jesse stood looking at his feet. "Sorry, sir. It won't happen again."

Mr. Livingston stiffened, then relaxed and shook his head. "Good. Find a seat."

Jesse sauntered around Livingston and sat in the last open seat in front of Cisco. They nodded at each other, and Jorge gave Jesse a fist bump.

"Hey, do you have an extra pen or pencil?"

Chase looked up to find Grácia Davis six inches from his face. A waft of fragrance made him feel a little dizzy.

"Yeah, sure," he said, trying not to jump out of his skin. He reached down into his backpack to rummage around for a pen.

"Here you go," he said, using the coolest voice he could muster. Grácia thanked him, then spun around to face the front of the room. When her hair brushed across his face, the smell was intoxicating. He took a deep breath and closed his eyes. Music started playing in his mind. *"Wild Thing," Fancy, 1974*, he thought.

> *"What kind of shampoo do you use?" he asked Grácia.*
>
> *She smiled broadly. The room was different. She wasn't wearing her school uniform anymore, but a crazy 1970s floral.*
>
> *She beamed even brighter, like a soft focus, old movie close-up. "Organic tea tree oil with lavender extracts," she answered. "Why do you ask?"*
>
> *He took a deep breath. "Because your hair smells spectacular!" Now he noticed everyone in the room, including himself, was wearing '70s clothing.*
>
> *"I know! Right?" She leaned in toward him coyly.*
>
> *He nudged her arm. "Why you smilin' at me?"*
>
> *"'Cause!" she quipped. "Do you want to dance?"*
>
> *"Sure!"*
>
> *The volume went up in his head. "Wild thing . . . you make my heart sing . . ."*

Chase's eyes closed, and he hummed to himself as Livingston continued to lecture. Grácia turned and looked at him briefly. He was in his own world.

At the front of the room Mr. Livingston continued. "The First Amendment of the Bill of Rights stipulates," he read from his notes, "'Congress shall make no law respecting an establishment of religion, or prohibiting the free exercise thereof; or abridging the freedom of speech, or of the press; or the right of the people peaceably to assemble, and to petition the government for a redress of grievances.' Why would the architects of the American Constitution insist on something like this? Of all things, why would this be the first amendment they would make to the Constitution?"

"'Cause we're the land of the free, dude!" Jorge shot out.

"Right," Mr. Livingston shot back, "but please, George, don't call me 'dude.'" Although Jorge's name was a traditional Hispanic name, he insisted everyone call him *George*. Why? "Because it's phonetic, dude!" was Jorge's retort. It didn't make sense, but it stuck.

"Yeah, sure, dude!"

Mr. Livingston raised his eyebrows.

Jorge blanched. The class laughed.

"I mean, yes, sir, Mr. Livingston." Then, lowering his voice so only those closest could hear him, he punctuated it with another "dude."

Mr. Livingston nodded and continued. "As George so aptly pointed out, it is indeed about freedom, but there's even more beneath that. It's also about individuality and human dignity. It's about respecting others and their ideas. It's about our unalienable rights to 'life, liberty, and the pursuit of happiness.' Freedom of speech without a respectful forum for debate is chaos.

"You will, from time to time, have to debate topics in this class that you feel personally passionate about. However, I require that during this process, regardless of our personal feelings, we stay respectful of one another. There is an old saying: 'Beware the sound of one hand clapping.' If there's an argument on one side, there's bound to be an argument on the other as well—and both deserve to be heard.

"Primarily, debate is about finding the truth, yes." Mr. Livingston nodded toward OB. "But it is also about creating a forum in which all voices can be respectfully heard. It's about giving even minority opinions the right to be considered so that all the facets of a topic are scrutinized before we decide what that truth actually is. Debate is about arguing in a civilized manner using dialectic reasoning as the guiding principle—without emotion or prejudice—because no one truth has the right to silence any other."

Chase heard Jorge lean over and whisper to Cisco, "What's dialectic reasoning?"

"Using logic to expose false beliefs, knucklehead," Cisco whispered back. Cisco sat at the back of the room, but he was nobody's fool. He was always listening and he didn't miss a beat.

"Oh yeah, I knew that!" Jorge retorted.

Another whiff of Grácia's hair floated toward Chase. His eyes closed again, and his humming grew louder. Chase's thoughts were a million miles away.

As if from the far end of a tunnel, Mr. Livingston kept speaking. Then he said, "Lastly, debate improves our ability to listen, authentically, when other people are presenting their views." He stepped from behind his lectern and began walking toward Chase as his humming continued. OB knew this wasn't going to end well, but he had no way to nudge Chase back to reality from where he sat.

Chase's desk suddenly shook. "Isn't that right, Mr. Morgan?"

Chase's eyes popped open. The whole class was staring at him, and Mr. Livingston had both hands on his desk, looking directly into his face. He was about as far away as Grácia had been when she asked for a pen.

The bell rang.

"Yes, Mr. Livingston," Chase answered.

The class broke into laughter as people started collecting their things. Some kids were shaking their heads. They'd seen all this before.

Mr. Livingston smiled dimly and slapped Chase on the arm, then went back to the front of the room.

"Thanks for your pen." Grácia held it out to him, smiling sympathetically.

"Uh, yeah," he said, taking it. "You're welcome."

He put his things away as quickly as he could and left without looking back.

THREE
PKS, BEARS, AND SUMMER CAMP

John Livingston stood pouring himself a cup of coffee. "Does this year's senior class seem weaker to you? I'm not sure what I'm going to do with the bunch I've got this first semester."

Zach Brady sat at a table nearby, sorting through what his wife had made him for lunch. They were in the teachers' lounge, where they usually had lunch together. A couple of other teachers sat on the couch and chairs facing each other on the other side of the room. The PE teacher was on his cell phone, and an English teacher was taking notes in the margins of a novel while balancing a salad on her lap. Bridgett Stevens sat in a chair about halfway between the two groups, strumming her guitar.

Zach looked at John skeptically. His eyebrows furrowed. "Not for a master teacher like you!" he prodded. "Even Jesse Valentine is nothing for a master like you."

John ignored the comment. "Bobbi . . ." His face crinkled. "What's her name?"

"Ryan?" Zach offered. "The one Valentine's going out with?"

"Yeah." John nodded. He took his coffee and found a seat on the other side of the table from Zach. "She seems bright. What's she see in a guy like that?"

Zach thought for a moment. "Well, maybe she's drawn to his 'bad boy' image."

"Why would you think that?" John countered.

"Well, her dad's a pastor."

"Okay, now you've completely lost me. What would that have to do with anything? Wouldn't that mean just the opposite?"

Zach was only half-listening, distracted by Bridgett's playing. "Wow, you've gotten a lot better over the summer."

"Unbelievable!" John countered.

"Why, thank you!" Bridgett said.

John shot her a look. "I'm talking about Bobbi's dad. What's his being a pastor have to do with her making bad choices in her love life?"

"Give her a break," she said. "It's tough being a PK."

John's face twisted into even more confusion. "A *what*?"

Zach chimed in, "A pastor's kid."

Bridgett picked up his train of thought. "PKs usually get a bad rep. In fact, my best friend growing up was one. Her dad was stretched in too many directions with all his responsibilities at the church. Everyone got his attention but her. With her dad not being around much, she stopped hanging out with our group of friends and started hanging with a sketchy crowd. The church talked about her behind her back, and that pushed her further away. Before we knew it, she was against everything her dad stood for. It's a sad stereotype, but unfortunately, it tends to fit more often than not."

John shook his head and decided to switch gears. "Speaking of religious kids"—he looked at Zach—"your buddy Chase Morgan was doing that zoning-out thing again." Livingston closed his eyes and started to hum "Wild Thing."

"Wait, I know that!" Zach squeezed his eyes tightly as he tried to find the tune in his head. "'Wild Thing'!" he blurted out, opening his eyes.

"Nineteen sixty-five," Bridgett said knowingly.

John nodded. "But it didn't become a big hit until Fancy rerecorded it in '74."

"Nah," Bridgett said. "The Troggs' version made it to number one in 1966!"

Like a quiz show emcee, Zach asked, "How long was it on Billboard's top 100?"

"Which version?" Bridgett asked.

"Fancy's, of course," he shot back.

"I think it was . . ." Bridgett paused. "Forty-two weeks?"

"Close," John cut in. "Forty-four, to be precise."

Zach looked at Bridgett consolingly. "He's right. Forty-four weeks."

She rolled her eyes. "I can't keep up with you two!"

To fight off any further remarks, she went back to playing her guitar. She started strumming the tune John had been humming and sang softly but passionately: "Wild thing . . . you make my heart sing . . ."

* * * * *

Chase sat at the lunch table, humming to himself and staring blankly into space, as OB walked up and sat down. OB took a big swig out of his juice box and it slurped loudly. "You know what frustrates me about juice boxes?" he said, holding it up to examine it. "You never know if you've sucked the last drop out of it. The straw hole is so small you can't see inside of it." He pulled out the straw and squinted, trying to see inside. "I hate that!" He put the straw back in and took another loud slurp, then sat it down, shaking his head.

Chase gave no response.

"Wild thing . . . I think I love you . . ."

"Earth to Chase!" OB reached across and snapped his fingers beside Chase's ears.

Chase opened his eyes.

"You're zoning out way too much lately."

Chase shrugged.

"You should get that checked out!"

Chase laughed. "You sound like my dad."

OB lifted his shoulders, trying to look imposing. In the best imitation he could do of Chase's father, he said, "What were you humming, son?"

"A song from the '70s."

"You're living in the past, man!" OB said incredulously.

"Don't you know it."

OB attempted another swig of his juice box. It was clearly empty now. "Ah! Nothing but air!" He put it down. "So, how was the hardware store this summer?"

"Okay." Chase shrugged.

"Your dad and you didn't kill each other working side by side?"

"Nope, although I did get a little tired of all the '70s tunes he sings day after day after day."

"Your dad is quite the guy. Gotta love his puns!"

"No," Chase said emphatically. "I don't!" He shook his head and decided to change the subject. "How was Yellowstone?"

OB looked at him seriously. "I need you to do me a favor as a friend."

"Hmm, sure," Chase agreed.

"Mark my words! I am never—*ever*—going camping with my family again. Hold me to it!"

Chase was confused. "Why not?"

"Okay, picture this—if you will—Yellowstone National Park. We're going camping—in a tent *made of nylon. Nylon,* Chase! We're parked in between campers that look like Fort Knox. My dad forgets to put the food in the cooler."

"He didn't!"

"Ah, he most definitely did! And *it's in our tent!*"

Chase's eyes widened.

"About 4:00 a.m., I hear—*snff, snff*—sniffling by my head."

"You didn't!"

"I did! Then, um—*snff, grrnt, snff, snff*—I, uh . . ." OB paused, looking for the right word. "*Soiled* myself."

"You didn't!" Chase was half-laughing now.

"*I did!* It was a bear, a *very* large bear. A very large, *hungry* bear, probably hungry enough to settle for whatever it found that was *edible.*" OB grew more emphatic. "He starts clawing at the tent—I'm not really sure what to do. I'm about to, like, open the zipper and make a run for it when suddenly—"

"Excuse me, do you mind if I join you?"

OB spun around as if he had heard the bear again, but it was the new girl. Chase looked at Grácia as if she were the bear.

OB was suddenly nonchalant. "Please!" He scooted to make room. "Join us!"

She put her tray down and sat.

Offering his hand, OB introduced himself. "I'm Obadiah Zechariah, but everybody calls me OB."

Grácia took his hand, shook it. "Nice! OB." As she sat down beside OB, she continued, "As you heard this morning, my name is Grácia—but please call me Grace."

OB and Grácia turned as one to look at Chase. He gave them a look that clearly demonstrated that he had no idea what they wanted.

OB shook his head. "And this is my mute friend, Chase Morgan."

Grácia smiled again—and Chase was lost again.

Only then did he realize that they had been expecting him to introduce himself. "Oh hi," he blurted. Then he looked away quickly, not knowing what to do next.

"So what's your story?" OB asked Grace.

She looked puzzled. "What do you mean?"

"You know. Where're you from? How did you end up here?"

"Oh." Grácia put her hand on her chest. "Is this an interview? Are you recording this?"

OB raised his eyebrows authoritatively. "Well, actually, in order to sit here, you have to answer a few skill-testing questions." He made air quotes around "skill-testing."

"Oh, okay. Well." Grace started pointing at each of her fingers, as if mentally reading off a list. "My dad's a microbiologist. Davis is an Irish name. My mom's an artist. She's Puerto Rican. They met in Florida when they were in college. My dad does research all over the globe, so I've lived practically everywhere."

"Oh, a woman of the world." OB sounded impressed. "So—how'd you get into Livingston's class? There's a lottery to get in that I'm pretty sure you weren't here last fall to get in on."

Now it was Grace's turn to raise her eyebrows. "Connections," she said knowingly. She winked at Chase.

Chase flushed. "Really?" His brow furrowed. She seemed to him like a girl who would have connections.

"No." She smiled broadly again, releasing the air of pretense. "When I registered yesterday they told me there was an opening. Someone dropped out just before I got there."

"Whoa! Nice timing!" OB dropped in.

Grace looked at OB, then fixed her eyes on Chase again. "Perfect timing," she said with another knowing look.

OB nodded to Chase for him to chime in.

Chase nodded back as if to say, *Keep this conversation going, OB. You're the one with the big mouth!* But OB wouldn't say anything. Finally Chase shook his head and looked at his iPhone. "Um, I actually think I've got to go."

"What's your hurry? We still have fifteen!" OB chided. He nodded sideways toward Grace, indicating, *Hello! Pretty girl alert! What could possibly be more important?*

Chase got to his feet and picked up his tray. "I need to talk to Mr. B. He wants to know how my summer went." He nodded at Grácia. "Nice meeting you, Grace." Then he spun and sped away. Before he got to the end of the table, he heard OB joke, "Yeah—he's, like, on lots of medication."

Grace giggled. "Seriously?"

OB shook his head. "No, but he should be!"

* * * * *

Amy Daniels sat alone. She picked at the lunch her mom had made her, watching Chase, OB, and the new girl laughing together. Something inside of her sank.

Suddenly Josie Fullerton and Zabrina Du Bois set their trays down on either side of her. "So, you like Tyler?" Josie's words were like an assault.

"Huh?" Amy was a deer caught in headlights.

Zabrina laughed. There was menace in her tone. Amy turned to Zabrina and felt her shoulders tense.

Josie gave Amy a once-over. Innocence personified, she thought. Still. She hadn't learned anything over the summer after hanging out with the two of them. Josie sometimes wondered why they'd bothered to latch on to her at the end of the previous school year. Then she remembered, It's always good to have a patsy around.

Josie and Zabrina sat down. "Don't play Snow White with me," Josie went on. "I saw you and Tyler checking each other out in Livingston's class this morning. I thought maybe you thought he was cute. But I realize now you didn't know he and I were going out . . ."

Amy was completely lost. "Oh, no, I don't think . . ."

"So you don't think my boyfriend is cute, then?" The edge of accusation was back.

"Oh, no, I—yes, of course he's cute, but I didn't mean . . . which one is he?"

Josie clicked her tongue. "Isn't she adorable, Z?"

"Precious," Zabrina said. She looked at Amy as if she were ready to eat her alive. She'd been working on it all summer and liked the effect her vampirish look seemed to have on Amy.

After an uncomfortably long moment, Josie finally broke the silence. "What are we going to do with this girl of ours, Z?" She put her arm around Amy. "I'm kidding, girl! You need to relax and take a joke. Tyler means nothing to me."

Amy laughed with them uncomfortably. She looked over at OB and Grace sitting and enjoying each other's company and wondered what she had gotten herself into hanging out with these two.

* * * * *

Chase's mind raced as he made his way down the hallway and out of the building toward the staircase that led to Mr. B's room. *Twice in one day*, he thought. There was no accounting for his luck. *And she sat down at lunch with us?* It had to be a fluke. *She's new. She doesn't know anyone else. She'll find better friends before long.*

Better to just put her out of my mind.

Before he realized it, he was standing in the doorway to Mr. Brady's classroom.

"Chase! My man! How was your summer? How's the hardware business?"

"Uh . . ." Chase stammered, as if Mr. Brady had just popped in on him, and not the other way around. "Hey, Mr. B! Um, good—and good! How was your summer?"

"It was really good, Chase. Alisha's walking now. It was great to have the time off and just be a dad, you know?"

Chase liked kids, but he hadn't spent much time around babies. "I guess."

Zach Brady laughed. "You'll know someday, Chase. Believe me. I don't think I understood it much myself until Alisha was born."

Chase smiled uncomfortably.

"So, did you do anything else this summer besides work?" Mr. Brady offered as a way out of his awkwardness.

"Not much," Chase answered. Then he thought about it. "I did go to camp."

"Summer camp! I remember summer camp! I think some of the most important moments of my life before college happened at church camp." Mr. Brady looked a little nostalgic for a moment. "Any crazy adventures? Did you have a good speaker? Meet any cute girls? Pull any awesome pranks?" His face brightened with mischief.

Chase looked at the floor again. "I dunno."

"Come on," Mr. Brady prodded. "You can tell me. It's just us guys here."

Chase shrugged again. "It was fun and all . . ."

"Yes?"

"I dunno. It's just that you go up to camp like that, you get all excited about stuff, then you come back and nothing is really different. You hear the speakers, you feel like God is so close, so real, but then you come back home and it's like it all washes off the first time you take a shower."

"Mm-hmm." Mr. B nodded. Then he looked expectantly at Chase, waiting for him to go on.

"I dunno," Chase said for a third time. "It's just that you get so emotionally charged to change things, and then it's gone. The speaker challenged us to make a difference in the world." Chase let out a small laugh.

"That's funny?" Mr. B asked.

"Well, no, but, I mean . . . What does he expect? Even if I really wanted that to happen—even if I really wanted to make a difference—it ain't happening with me. I'm not that kind of person. I mean, what does he think is going to happen? We're all gonna go back to our hometowns and turn our schools upside down, convert everyone. That's not gonna happen here." Chase looked directly at Mr. B for the first time since he'd come in. "He really thinks some lame high-school kid is going to go home and change the world? Is he naive, or just trying to be over the top so he'll be asked to speak at more camps?"

Mr. B shook his head. "You're talking to the wrong person if you want me to agree with any of that." He looked around at some of the posters on his wall. "I'm a history teacher, remember? History is full of people who took a stand and started a movement. It's full of people—individuals—who championed a cause and made a difference. They spoke out with a clear voice and got people to listen. They stood up for those who couldn't stand up for themselves. They got people to see what was wrong in their societies and what needed to change.

"People like William Wilberforce, who fought his whole life to end slavery in the British Empire. Thomas Edison, who had one successful experiment in thousands to create the light bulb and give people more hours in their day. Rosa Parks, who refused to sit in the back of the bus and fought against segregation in America. Gutenberg, who took a winepress, block letters, ink, and paper to revolutionize the way people learned. Clara Barton, a young nurse, who started the Red Cross and helped provide emergency relief to millions and millions.

"Chase, change almost always starts with just one person—usually with one person who finds their voice and is willing to stand up for what they believe."

Chase shook his head. "I dunno, Mr. B. It can't be that simple—"

"Oh, I didn't say it was simple, Chase. I just said it usually started with one person. It's usually anything but simple."

Chase's face broke into a wry smile. "You sound a lot like that speaker, Mr. B. You ever thought of being a preacher?"

"Who says I'm not?" Mr. B shot back.

The bell rang.

Chase looked at him confused for a moment, then seemed to get it. "Yeah, I guess you do kinda talk like that in class too," he said. He laughed weakly, as if something just occurred to him. "Well, anyway, it ain't happening with me—"

"I wouldn't be so sure." Zach Brady smiled and punched him in the arm. "There's a lot more to you than you realize."

Chase looked confused again.

"Get to class," Mr. Brady told him. "I'll see you seventh period."

FOUR
FIRST NIGHT

Firelight flickered across Jesse's face in the dark living room. Bobbi smiled. It felt good to have him so close, but there was always a strange sting to it as well. He leaned in to kiss her again, and she felt his hand wandering, trying to work its way between her belt line and the edge of her T-shirt.

She took his hand in hers and turned away.

Jesse stopped. "Bobbi, what's wrong?"

Bobbi stared into the fire. Jesse looked at her intensely. Trying not to lose momentum, he brushed her hair gently from off her neck with the hand she wasn't holding and kissed her on the nape.

Bobbi stiffened. Jesse sat back up.

She took both of his hands in hers this time and looked at them. Then she looked up into his eyes. "Jesse, I've been thinking. Are you okay with this?"

"Okay? This rates way higher than okay!" He leaned over to kiss her neck again.

Bobbi put her hand on his chest to stop him. "No, what I mean is, is *this* okay?"

Jesse's face darkened with confusion. "I don't follow." Then he leaned back toward her.

"Can you *stop* for a moment?" she said sharply.

"Hmm?"

"Jess, I'm a Christian."

He took a deep breath and sat back into the couch. "I know that." He reached over and started rubbing her shoulder.

"As a Christian I'm not supposed to . . ." She fell silent.

"I'm listening, babe."

". . . have sex." She stumbled over the word. "I mean, before I get married."

Jesse feigned surprise. "I don't see anyone having sex here, do you?" He started looking around the room as if he hadn't realized someone else was there.

Bobbi laughed and punched him softly. "Okay, can you stop joking?" She took his face in both hands and looked into his eyes. "I'm being serious. Are you listening to a word I'm saying?"

Jesse tried to look somber. "Absolutely. You're talking about sex—and not doing it." He looked her squarely in the eye and shrugged. "And stuff like that." Jesse smiled, took her hand, and looked at it.

Her smile vanished and her brow furrowed. "So where do you stand in all this?"

Jesse was leaning back toward her neck while she was pausing, and the question caught him. "To be honest with you, I haven't put much thought into it. I don't know. I just do what comes natural." He nuzzled his face into her neck again, like a puppy wanting attention.

Bobbi shouldered him away and looked into his face. "You don't feel any guilt?"

Jesse shook his head. He looked into her eyes deeply. "Guilt would definitely not express what I'm feeling right now."

Bobbi sat back into the arm of the couch and looked at him. "Then what are you feeling?"

Jesse leaned forward, took both of her hands in his, and kissed them. "Unbelievably attracted to the most beautiful woman I know."

A big grin spread across Bobbi's face, but she turned away.

Jesse put his hand on his heart. "Honest to God!"

"I thought you didn't believe in God."

Jesse looked at her with that coy look she'd seen so many times before. "You're making me a believer, baby! You're making me a believer."

Bobbi laughed and then locked eyes with Jesse. In an instant, she was lost in them again. Before she realized it, they were kissing passionately.

Headlights flashed through the window.

Jesse's head shot around. "What's that?"

Bobbi turned toward the window and recognized the sound of the family minivan. "Great! My parents are home early." A hot rush of guilt flooded inside her, and for a second she felt overwhelmed. Then she felt a slight twinge of gratitude they hadn't been left alone a minute more. She batted both feelings away.

Jesse's eyes widened. "What are we gonna do?"

Bobbi looked at the light switch, wondering if she could get to it before her parents came in. No good. Then an idea popped into her head. She got down on her knees and folded her hands on the couch. "Kneel down."

"*What?*"

"Kneel down beside me. Hurry up." Bobbi pulled him down beside her. "Bow your head." Bobbi bowed her head and closed her eyes. In a voice a little louder than was natural, she said, "And Lord, keep Jesse safe as he drives home tonight . . ."

The lights came on. She heard her father's voice. "That's odd—the lights are off. I thought Bobbi was home."

A little louder still. "And help all those out on the roads to get home safely . . . Oh!" Bobbi opened her eyes and tried to act surprised. "Hi, Mom—Dad. Jesse and I were just praying."

Jesse ducked further down into the couch.

"In the dark?" Bobbi's dad asked, making no effort to keep the cynicism out of his voice.

"Yeah," Bobbi answered, unshaken. "We find it easier to concentrate on praying when the lights are off. Right, Jesse?"

Jesse kept his eyes tightly closed until Bobbi elbowed him.

"*Right*, Jesse?"

He looked up but didn't make eye contact with anyone. "Yeah, it's way better in the dark."

"Really?" Bobbi's dad didn't sound any more convinced. He looked at his wife for help. She didn't return his gaze, but was looking at Jesse with a bemused grin on her face. She had no doubt about what had actually been going on, and here was her husband scolding Bobbi and Jesse for doing the exact same thing they'd done as teenagers two decades ago. *What goes around comes around,* she thought.

Silence hung awkwardly in the air.

"Well, um—I should probably get goin'." Jesse got to his feet and grabbed his hoodie off the arm of the couch. "Guess I'll see you later, Bobbi."

"Bye, Jesse," she responded.

He nodded and then brushed past Bobbi's dad, patting his shoulder without looking at him. "Pastor Ryan." He scooted out the door as quickly as he could.

"Take care, Jesse," Mrs. Ryan called after him. She turned to her daughter, ready to say something, then stopped herself.

Pastor Ryan hadn't taken his eyes off his daughter the entire time. "Bobbi?" he said, with a twinge of anger and disappointment. In his mind's eye he still saw his daughter as a twelve-year-old babbling at the dinner table about something that happened at school. He'd felt he knew what he was doing as a father then. Now he wasn't so sure.

There was a knock at the door. Pastor and Mrs. Ryan both turned.

The door opened. "Sorry, I forgot my shoes." Jesse fumbled past Mrs. Ryan to grab them.

Bobbi couldn't help but giggle.

"Drive safely, Jesse," Mrs. Ryan said.

"Go home, Jesse." Pastor Ryan made no effort to keep the frustration out of his voice.

"Um, I'm gonna go to bed. It's late," Bobbi said.

"Bobbi . . ." Her father spoke as if out of breath. It came out softer and more exasperated than he had meant it to. Bobbi stood and headed for the hallway.

Pastor Ryan regained his composure and spoke firmly. "Bobbi, your mother and I would like to talk to you." Turning toward her, he emphasized, *"Now!"*

Bobbi stopped in her tracks and rolled her eyes before turning around. Mrs. Ryan looked worried, and Pastor Ryan's face was a storm.

Taking exaggerated, slow steps, Bobbi crossed back to the sofa and then collapsed into it, hands clasped. She looked at the fire and hoped whatever happened next didn't last forever.

* * * * *

Amy Daniel's phone vibrated a third time with another message as she got off of the bus at the stop near her house. "K. Meet us by my locker before Livingston's. CYA!"

Her cheeks warmed momentarily, even as she felt a slight queasiness in her stomach. She didn't trust Josie and Zabrina, but she liked the attention. Besides, it had been nice not to have to go straight home to a lonely house after school. She looked at the time on her phone: 7:46. She checked the message thread to her mom one more time. Amy's last message, "I'm gonna eat dinner with some friends at the mall. B home around 7:30," had been read, but there was no reply.

Amy made her way down the street toward her house. The sun had just dropped below the horizon, but it was going to be another warm, end-of-summer evening. Amy walked slowly. Even though it was later than she'd told her parents she would be there, she was in no rush. It was not as though they cared or anything.

Turning into her cul de sac, she could vaguely see that the lights in the back rooms of the house looked on, but the upstairs was dark. Out of habit she looked to the upstairs window on the far right, where she always used to see Billy playing or watching for her to come home. It was dark, too, of course. What had she expected? Regardless, she still felt a lump in her throat.

She picked up her pace and made her way down the street and through her front yard.

"Mom, I'm home!" she called as she came through the front door.

"Hi, sweetie!" she heard from the back of the house— probably the family room off of the kitchen where her mother was usually lost in a book. "Are you hungry?"

"No, I ate at the mall with Josie and Zabrina."

"Mmm-hmm, okay. Let me know if you want anything."

Amy closed the door behind her and waited, but nothing else came from the back. No questions about what she had been doing with Josie and Zabrina. Even though her mom knew who they were, she never asked about them.

"Dad home yet?" Amy called toward the back.

"No, working late—*again*." It was suppose to be a joke, but she sounded exasperated. "Are you sure you don't want a snack or something?"

Amy suppressed a smile. Like many Southern mothers, her mom applied food as if it could cure any ailment, physical or emotional. "Maybe later," Amy answered. "I'm gonna go study upstairs."

"Okay, sweetie. I'll check on you later."

Amy switched on the lights. The front room to her right was immaculate, as usual. They never really used the room except when they had guests, and other than cleaning it, no one had really gone into it since the funeral. Amy hardly gave it a glance as she made her way up the stairs, clicking on lights as she went. Nor did she give a glance to the pictures that lined the wall as she ascended. Year after year of family pictures: her mom and dad, her beautiful blond-haired older sister, Amy, and an ever-smiling young boy with Down syndrome—her little brother, Billy.

The front of the second floor was divided into three bedrooms. Chelsea—who was away at college—had the room on the left, Amy's was in the middle, and the one that had been Billy's was at the end of the hall across from her parents'. All the doors were closed. Immediately to her left, at the top of the stairs, was a sort of upstairs family or TV room with a full bar that was her father's pride and joy. She flipped the light on and threw her backpack on one of the sectionals, then went to the fridge behind the bar. She took a coconut water from the middle shelf and made her way back over to collapse into the couch.

She dug her phone out of a side pocket of her pack and began flipping through the selfies she'd taken at the mall with Josie and Zabrina: getting coffees at Starbucks with the hunk of a barista in the background; trying on clothes at Forever 21; Zabrina trying to drop French fries on one of the security guards; and the three of them with the four LSU guys Josie somehow knew. Josie had convinced Amy to give one of them her phone number. The thought made her flush.

Amy had never even talked to any college guys before, let alone given one her phone number. The truth was, every time she hung out with Josie and Zabrina was a mix of excitement and dread. She felt giddy at the thought of that boy calling sometime, even while uneasiness clawed at her stomach. She wasn't sure what to make of it.

Near the end of the year before she'd struck up an awkward conversation with them when they cornered her at her locker. They were far more sophisticated and boy crazy than she was, but she was strangely drawn to them. Maybe it was their air of sophistication or their edginess, but she liked being with Josie and Zabrina even if she was always scared of what they might do next. As the summer wore on, she hung out with them more—and by the time school started, she was part of the posse. She smiled to herself and started flipping through her pictures again to see if she could find the one of her and the guy she'd given her number to.

Her phone chirped, and she opened the message from her mom. "You ready for that snack?"

"I'm okay. Gonna study now," she replied.

"Okay. Love you, sweetie. Let me know if you want anything. I'll just be down here reading. XOXOXO."

"Love U2," she messaged back.

She opened Instagram and started flipping through pictures to see if Josie or Zabrina had posted any from the afternoon. The light of a smile brightened her face with each new post she found. Just a couple of pictures, but they had tagged her in each one.

She sighed, then touched the search box and typed in "Chase Morgan." He was, of course, the first entry it pulled up. She selected his name and saw he hadn't posted for a couple of weeks, so she tapped his pictures and started looking through the ones he'd shared from summer camp. She sighed again, a bit more deeply this time, and slowly flipped from one picture to the next.

* * * * *

"Mom! I'm home!" OB burst through the door into the house and dropped his backpack on the floor by a wall rack of coats. "What's for dinner?"

OB trudged down the hall to find his mom cooking in the kitchen, just where he always found her when he came home after practice. He breathed in deeply. "Hmm, chili? Did you make cornbread too?"

His mother didn't turn around from stirring the pot. "Yes, of course, silly." She lifted the spoon to her mouth to give it a taste. "Just the way you like it, I think." She scooped up a bigger spoonful and offered it to him. "Here, give it a try."

OB nearly swallowed the spoon. He chewed, then opened his mouth in an "O" shape and sucked in a breath. "Nice. Tangy." He waved his hand in front of his mouth.

His mom laughed. "Set the table, please. I need to keep an eye on the cornbread for another minute or so."

OB pulled three bowls, three plates, and the necessary silverware from the cupboard and drawers. "Where's Dad?"

"He's out in the shed getting things ready for tomorrow. He's starting in that new subdivision up in Brownfields tomorrow. He should be in soon."

OB nodded and started setting things out on the table.

* * * * *

Bobbi's mom stood at the sink, rinsing dishes and putting them into the dishwasher. She worked quietly and somewhat stiffly, even though she usual hummed or sang softly to herself when working in the kitchen. Tonight she was quiet because she was listening. She couldn't make out the words from the living room, but she knew the volume was higher than it should be.

She heard footsteps and then a door closing firmly upstairs. She jumped slightly at the sound. Her husband's footsteps made their way heavily down the hallway. She took a deep breath, making a conscious effort to release the growing tension in her shoulders. Humming softly to herself, she forced her mouth into a smile.

Her husband came into the kitchen, flung open the refrigerator, pulled out a pitcher of tea, and almost slammed it down on the counter. She winced slightly. Then a cupboard banged open and she heard a glass land on the counter sharply. The cabinet shut and she heard tea pouring into the glass.

"Did you tell her that you loved her?" she asked.

"Hmm?"

With a dish in one hand and a sponge in the other, she turned around and sat against the lip of the counter in front of the sink. She consciously raised the edges of her mouth again, hoping it looked more like a smile than a grimace. "Before you finished talking to Bobbi—did you tell her that you loved her?"

He looked at her blankly, then furrowed his brow. "I'm sure I did." His eyes fell slightly, uncertain. "We always do." He took a shaky drink from his glass.

Mrs. Ryan's face warmed. "Are you okay?"

"Hmm?" he said again, looking up at his wife. "Oh, yes, I'll be okay. I just don't know what to do when she's like this."

"You two are so much alike."

Her husband looked confused. "What do you mean?"

"What? You don't think I remember you at that age? When we first started dating? Stubborn, rebellious, and angry."

"What in the world did you ever see in me?" Pastor Ryan said as he shook his head.

"Honestly," Mrs. Ryan said as she walked over to him and put her hands in his, "a determined, passionate, handsome man who was going to change the world!"

Pastor Ryan shook his head and pulled away. "It's just that boy—"

"Jim, she's your daughter. She's trying to figure it out. And he's just a mixed-up kid. Reminds me very much of someone I fell in love with at that age."

He cringed and shook his head. "No, no. He's not good for her. I don't know what she sees in him."

Mrs. Ryan's mouth gave a slight pout. "I do," she said, looking right at him. Her face broadened into a grin again.

"I don't see it." He crossed to the sink and placed his glass on the counter, then leaned over and gave his wife a kiss on the cheek. "I don't know how you ever fell in love with me." He wrapped his arms around her, squishing the plate and sponge to her chest.

"Careful, Pastor." She gave a playful look at the window. "The neighbors might be watching."

He stiffened slightly, let her go, and gave a furtive look out the window even though he knew she was joking. He gave her another kiss on the cheek and let out a sigh. "Men's prayer breakfast in the morning, six a.m. I better get to bed."

She leaned over and gave him a kiss full on the mouth. "I'll just finish up here and be up in a few minutes." She turned back to the sink.

* * * * *

"I love-a my espresso," Chase sang as he lifted the cup from the espresso machine he kept in his room. "I drink it all the more-a. It makes me so happy!" He took a sip. It was bitter and he made a face.

Skype chimed on his computer. It was OB. He answered it, and OB appeared on the screen, lying on his bed, trying to spin a football on his finger.

"Hello, Guv'nah," OB greeted in his mock British accent. "How was your first day?"

Chase shrugged, raised his eyebrows, and pursed his lips noncommittally. "Decent. Yours?"

"Decent," OB agreed. Chase was getting so lame lately. He tried again. "What'd *you* think of debate?" He pointed at the screen with the football to emphasize *you*.

"I don't know." Chase crinkled his forehead. "Livingston's going to be tough."

That's not what OB was asking about. "So?"

"So?"

"What do you think of *her*?"

"Who?" Chase pretended not to follow.

"Dude! Seriously?"

Chase gave in. "Grace?" He pressed his lips together again, as if he'd only now thought about her. "She's nice."

"That's it?"

Chase resettled himself uncomfortably and dropped the pretense. "What did you think?"

"She's cute."

"Yeah."

"That smile."

Chase repressed a sigh. "For sure."

OB pointed at his head. "Smart."

"True."

"And those eyes."

They sighed together.

Then, realizing they were acting like a couple of tween girls talking about a boy band, Chase coughed and changed the subject. "So, you do the assignment for Johnson's class?"

"Ah, *dude*, what assignment?"

"OB-Wan!"

"*Dude!*"

"I'll text it to you."

"Thanks, bro." He paused, trying to think of a clever comeback. "I *owe-B*-you-one!"

"Again," Chase said with emphasis. He closed the chat window, picked up his phone, checked his class notes, and started typing the assignment to send to OB.

FIVE
SCHOOL DAZE

Things became routine for Chase a bit too quickly after that first day. Except for Mr. Livingston's and Mr. B's classes, the rest seemed like any other year—English comp, calculus, Spanish 2, et cetera, et cetera, blah, blah, blah. Sure, his classes were a little harder, but Chase could get through most of them without having to say much. Most days he felt like he was sleepwalking between first and seventh periods with a brief intermission somewhere in between for lunch. It didn't help much either that he'd get a tune or a thought stuck in his head and drift off, often forgetting where he was until a bell or the call of his name brought him back to reality.

As he had expected, Grácia did move on to make other new friends. Maybe it was more accurate to say that she got swept up in her own activities—activities that, except for debate, didn't include Chase or OB. That didn't keep Chase from feeling like he saw her everywhere he went, though. Or was Chase just strangely showing up in places where he suspected she might be? He picked her out at lunch every day, hanging with various groups, including Cisco, Jorge, and some of the popular kids. For some reason, though, she never seemed to quite become one of them. Grace's and Chase's lockers weren't that far from one another in the senior hallway, so he almost always saw her between classes as well.

Apparently Grace had signed up as a volunteer tutor for math and writing, so Chase "just happened" to see her when he was studying in the library as she sat and helped different students. It never occurred to him as odd that he suddenly found the library a great place to study when he'd hardly ever spent any time there before. While Grace was on the volleyball team and Chase was on the cross-country team, somehow he always caught at least a glimpse of her when he cruised by the gym on the way to and from the track—even though it was quicker and easier to cut out the back door of the locker room.

Of course, whenever he saw her, she always seemed to catch him looking at her and shot him a quick smile. He could never quite get it out of his mind. Her smile had a way of popping into his memory at the oddest of moments as well, sort of how the Cheshire Cat's grin appeared to Alice. Without even realizing it, he kept looking for little excuses to see that smile whenever he could.

Chase usually fell into a fall funk soon after school started each year. He missed the summertime and the freedom of getting off work at the hardware store. He'd loved having money in his pocket and no commitments aside from going back to work the next day. But this year was definitely different. Whether he acknowledged it or not, seeing Grace everywhere gave him something to look forward to, in spite of the monotony of one class crashing into another.

He was back to the old routine—up early, classes, lunch, more class, cross-country practice, homework, sleep, repeat. Then again, somehow it was different—a difference punctuated by various instances of that warm, friendly, ready-to-take-on-the-world smile.

* * * * *

If one thing drew Bobbi to Jesse, it was that he made her laugh. Jesse never seemed serious about anything, while everything in Bobbi's world growing up seemed drenched in importance. Everything had a purpose, every activity chosen for its moral impact on the future, every conversation centered on becoming a better person in the eyes of God. Nothing else was tolerated. Bobbi never understood until she met Jesse how smothering that could feel.

For Bobbi, Jesse represented a sort of freedom. That her dad didn't have a grid for where Jesse fit into his plans for Bobbi somehow made him even better. Her dad always stumbled over himself trying to control his temper when he spoke about Jesse. That strange imbalance in her dad made Bobbi feel as though she could speak up for what she wanted, even if she didn't really know what it was. It felt like an opening in the chain-link fence—a place through which she could get out and experience the world that was beyond her father's control. Her mom, on the other hand, seemed to like Jesse. She often told Bobbi that he reminded her of Bobbi's father when they first started dating, though Bobbi had no idea how that could be true. To her, they seemed as different as night and day.

Jesse didn't bring a three-point sermon for how to be a better person to every conversation they shared. He had no pretense; he just was. He existed totally in a world of play, fun, and goofiness. She only had to think of him in the midst of one of his antics to feel more alive. Even though they'd been together for a year and a half, he still surprised her. And it felt good that he never expected her to be anyone but herself. He liked who she was. Jesse wasn't trying to mold her into something else. It felt good to just belong, to be flirted with, to be held and kissed, to be wanted.

Since school had started, though, things had begun to change. Bobbi couldn't really put her finger on what was different. Slowly she had grown to want more out of the relationship, even though she didn't know what that *more* was. The longer they went out, the more she felt as if Jesse was slipping away. The joking and playfulness seemed like avoidance rather than flirtation, and Jesse seemed to be buried behind layers she was never allowed to peel away. The more time she spent with Jesse, the less she felt she knew him—or that he knew her.

Bobbi was conflicted. She felt sorry for Jesse—he seemed like a lost puppy sometimes—but on the other hand, she knew she was playing with fire as they became more physical. She sensed that behind the jokes, Jesse hurt. Maybe that was part of why he needed her, though he'd never said anything like that, of course. Bobbi knew his dad had walked out on him and his mom when Jesse was entering seventh grade, and that his mom, though caring when she was around, was as wrapped up in her work as anyone Bobbi had ever met. Jesse's mom worked at a big law firm downtown and had dreamed of being the first woman partner of a very old-school, boys' club–type partnership—and she was going to break its glass ceiling even if it killed her. Bobbi liked her, but she also saw how her ambitions consumed her and left very little of herself to invest in Jesse. Over the time Bobbi had been with Jesse, she'd watched him and his mom growing further and further apart. Jesse's mom would smile and say that Jesse was becoming more and more like his dad every day, but under that smile, Bobbi sensed that wasn't completely a good thing.

Bobbi had never met Jesse's dad. He'd stayed in town and had been involved in Jesse's life until just before she met Jesse. But sometime in the first half of that year, his dad had moved to California with a twentysomething he'd met. As far as she could tell, and from what she could learn from Jesse, he'd left and never looked back. But then again, it was not as if it was a topic she could get Jesse to say much about.

What she did know was that Jesse didn't like being compared with his dad—and even though Bobbi didn't realize it, who Jesse was becoming scared his mom more than a little.

* * * * *

"Honey, can we talk?"

Bobbi's mom stood at the door to her room as Bobbi sat on her bed. She was flipping through *A Brave New World*, trying to figure out a good topic to write on. "Sure, Mom, what's up?" *Anything to put that off a little longer.*

Her mom's cheeks crinkled the way they did when she was concerned. "Frankly?" she said. "You and Jesse."

Bobbi rolled her eyes. "Mom! I'm seventeen! It's my life! I'm not a kid anymore! You and Dad can't expect—"

Her mother held up her hands in a gesture of surrender. "I'm not here to be critical," she said. "I see a lot of potential in Jesse. You know that." She paused for a beat. "I want to talk about you."

Bobbi suddenly felt really interested in Huxley's writing again. "Mom, I'm fine. You don't need to worry about me." She wished her mom would leave and let her get back to her homework.

"You really like him, don't you?" her mother asked evenly, remembering to smile. "The way you laugh when he gets all goofy—and I see the way you look at him sometimes . . ." Her voice trailed off.

Bobbi's expression softened. A shy smile snuck across her face as she thought about Jesse. "He just makes me feel—I don't know. Fun . . . free . . ."

Her mother came into the room and sat down on the edge of her bed. She looked into her daughter's eyes, smiling. "You didn't answer my question. Do you like him?"

Bobbi reddened. "Of course I do, Mom."

"Do you think that you love him?"

Bobbi looked at her feet, then out the window. "I think so, Mama," she answered without looking back. "I really do."

Her mother smiled. "I remember what that was like," she assured her. "It's both nice and terrifying at the same time."

Bobbi laughed uncomfortably. "Why is it like that?"

Her mother shook her head. "I don't know. God does have a sense of humor, after all." She smiled again. "But I think it's always because it's what we were created for and what we are afraid of at the same time."

"What do you mean?"

"Well," she said, stopping to think, "God is love. He created us out of love and made us capable of loving him back. He made us capable of loving each other." She paused again. "But we're not as we were when he created us. Love is both a calling into who we are becoming and out of who we are afraid we really are on the inside. Love makes us vulnerable. When we love, we risk letting someone know who we see ourselves to be, and that scares us because we aren't always sure we like who we *really* are. We're afraid that if the one we think we love sees us as we see ourselves, well . . . they'll only see our flaws. It's hard to really love someone until you know who you are." Her mom gave a weak smile. "I'm sorry, but that's hard to do when you are only seventeen." She reached out and pulled her daughter into a hug.

Bobbi thought about this for a moment, and then leaned away and looked at her mother. "Why did you say 'who we think we love'?"

"Well, because I don't think you're sure about it. Are you?"

"I don't know," Bobbi said. "I think I am . . ." When she heard herself say it out loud, she saw what her mother meant and laughed nervously.

"And do you think he loves you?" her mother ventured.

Bobbi looked into her mom's face, her eyes glistening. "I don't know."

Her mom reached over and put a hand on her leg. She was quiet for a moment. "You two were getting kind of physical the other night—"

"Mom!"

"Oh, I'm sorry. I thought I was talking to an adult." She started to stand up.

"Mom, don't." Bobbi shook her head and wiped an eye. "I'm sorry."

Her mother sat back down. "I know it's hard to talk about," she said. "Especially with your *mom*." She made a goofy face, and they both laughed a little. She patted her daughter's foot this time. "I could never talk with my mom about it. That's for sure," she confided.

Bobbi looked up, eyes still glistening.

"I just want you to know it's easy to get carried away with things. If you let it go too far . . ." Bobbi's mom hesitated, looked at the floor, then back to her daughter. "It's easy to get swept up in it."

"Mom, that won't happen," Bobbi said, a little too fast.

"It's really better not to start if you don't know—"

"Mom," Bobbi said more adamantly, "it's—not—going —to—happen!"

Mrs. Ryan could tell her daughter's walls were up again, and she wondered if she'd overstepped.

She patted her daughter's leg again, then looked back into her eyes. "I sure hope not, honey."

She stood up and walked out of her daughter's room, a lump growing in her throat. Bobbi eyes blazed under the glisten. Then she got up, closed her door, and fell back down onto her bed face-first, burying her head in a pillow.

* * * * *

Jorge sat on one of the "hot seat" stools used by debaters in Mr. Livingston's class. "My fellow students, I'm here to talk to you about a subject I know well: marijuana."

The class broke out in laughter, but Mr. Livingston was clearly not amused. "Ladies and gentlemen, settle down. This is a serious debate in several states now! We need to treat it with decorum. George, let's keep things mature, okay?"

Jorge nodded. Cisco winked at him, almost breaking him back into hysterics.

But Jorge regained his composure but slumped into the seat. "As a recreational drug, marijuana is way safer than tobacco or alcohol. For too long marijuana has been vilified as a gateway drug. Like, what does that even mean?" Jorge looked down at the index cards he held in his hands. "According to WHO—*WHO?*—wait, no . . ." He looked at his cards again. "I mean, according to the World Health Organization—"

A few students giggled, but Mr. Livingston glared in the direction of the culprits.

"According to the World Health Organization, more than six million die from tobacco-related illnesses every year, and more than 2.5 million deaths are related to alcohol. But get this: *No one's ever died from smoking weed.* I mean, from smoking marijuana!"

There was more laughter.

"People, settle down!"

Again things quieted. Mr. Livingston shot Jorge a look that said he was running out of patience.

Jorge sat up straighter and continued. "So tell me: Why is the possession of cannabis even considered a crime? Crimes are things that hurt people, but smoking a joint—I mean, marijuana—doesn't hurt anyone. In fact, it makes people more peaceful and generous. Look at me! No, wait, what I meant to say is . . . What was I saying?"

Several more people laughed. Mr. Livingston held up his hand, and the laughter died down once more. "George, let's stick to the facts, not opinions—and no more jokes."

Jorge was about to say something but caught himself. "Right, Mr. L." He gave him two thumbs up.

Jorge sorted through his index cards again and pulled one out. "Listen to this: a study in 2009 estimated that cannabis consumption is healthier than either of the legal drugs, tobacco or alcohol. Health costs for alcohol consumers are eight times higher than for cannabis users, and forty times higher for tobacco smokers. For people who want to relax and unwind after a hard day's work, smoking a joint or eating a brownie are both safer and healthier in the long run than either alcohol or tobacco."

Jorge was on a roll now. "And those are just some of the many reasons the benefits of marijuana outweigh the negatives." Then he broke into a goofy grin. "And speaking of brownies, is anyone else hungry?"

The class laughed.

"Thank you." Jorge stood and took a bow.

The class let out a controlled cheer and clapped. Mr. Livingston applauded weakly.

Grace looked on from where she'd been sitting on a stool on the opposite side of the lectern. Once the class quieted, Mr. Livingston nodded to her.

Grace stood and began, looking about the room and making eye contact with as many as possible. "Comparing marijuana to tobacco and alcohol leads to some false conclusions. First of all, current cannabis use is much lower than tobacco, so, yes: The health costs are much lower."

A football player in the front of the room smiled broadly, a little too intently focused on Grace. When she made eye contact with him as she did with several looking around the room, he winked. Grace pretended she didn't notice.

She walked over and leaned slightly on the lectern in the center of the room. "To say that marijuana is healthier than cigarettes might be true, but that is only an argument for keeping people from smoking. Not that marijuana is without its health risks.

"For one, the marijuana of today is not what was used for most of the testing in the past: It is four to five times stronger. For another, research more recent than 2009 has shown that cannabis can significantly decrease IQ—especially in teens; double the risk of automobile accidents; and significantly increase the risk of developing a mental illness. Marijuana users are also three times more likely to have thoughts of suicide."

Grace stood straight and walked across the front of the room, her hands folded like a lawyer addressing a jury. "More importantly for me, though, is why do we want to smoke marijuana or use cannabis to get high in the first place? Even if the drug were totally healthy—which it isn't—what is the appeal?"

She stopped pacing and looked around the room, letting the question hang in the air. "Most of the teens I know who use marijuana frequently do it to change their personal reality, to reduce pain or increase pleasure.

"I think all of us know someone whose life has been affected by it. The kid who used to be the all-star on your sports team who doesn't come to practice anymore . . ."

Mr. Livingston scanned the room and made eye contact with Jesse, who looked away.

"Or the straight-A student whose grades are starting to suffer . . . the loner no one pays attention to who drifts even further away . . . the new kid in school who does it a couple times at a party to fit in and is so filled with shame she starts fighting with her parents all of the time." She looked at Mr. Livingston. "Not to mention adults who feel pressure from work and or family and use it as a way to cope with life.

"There's compelling evidence that while marijuana use may not be more harmful to the user than cigarettes or alcohol, it harms us all. So, for these reasons I don't believe the benefits of marijuana outweigh the drawbacks. Thank you."

Grace sat back down on her stool to a weak ovation. She acknowledged it with a smile and a nod. Josie shot Amy a catty look, and Amy stopped clapping. Grace noticed this and looked at Josie questioningly. Josie returned her gaze with a glare just short of sticking out her tongue.

"Thank you, George, Grácia," Mr. Livingston said, rising from where he sat and coming to the lectern.

Jesse raised his hand.

"Mr. Valentine?" Mr. Livingston responded.

"Sir, what are your thoughts on pot?"

Cisco Diaz chuckled, and Jesse turned toward him. "Don't go there, Jess. Mr. L never shares his personal thoughts . . . *ever*."

Mr. Livingston smiled at Cisco in agreement and then addressed the class. "Voltaire said, and I'm paraphrasing here, 'I may not agree with what you have to say, but I will defend to the death your right to say it.' The freedom to share our convictions without fear is crucial, and nonnegotiable, if we are to call ourselves civilized."

The bell rang, and Mr. Livingston raised his voice as students began to leave. "We'll continue 'hot seat' on Monday. Have a great weekend!"

Several students circled Grace in the front, offering congratulations for her performance and asking questions. Chase watched her from his seat in the back of the room as OB came up beside him. They gave each other a fist bump. Sill looking at Grace, Chase said, "She's gotten more friends in three weeks than we've gotten in three years."

OB looked up at her. "What's she got," he patted his chest, "that we don't got?"

Chase looked at OB and then back at Grace. "Looks . . . charm . . . charisma . . . intelligence . . ."

"Okay, okay! I get it."

Chase got up and they headed for the door. "Personality . . . character . . . she probably doesn't fart in public . . ."

OB gave him a forearm to his side, almost knocking him over. They both laughed.

* * * * *

Grace finished up talking and returned to her seat to collect her notebooks. Then clutching them to her chest, she rushed to be sure to get to her next class on time. Just out the door, Josie, Zabrina, and Amy stood talking in a circle. As Grace tried to squeeze by, Zabrina nodded slightly and Josie turned as if leaving. She ran full into Grace, knocking her books out of her arms. "Oops. Sorry, Gray-*sha*."

Zabrina glared at Grace as she laughed, and Amy turned away.

Grace bent down and started picking up her things. "It's all right," she said, smiling at Josie. Once she had everything, she rushed down the hall past Chase, who had turned and seen it all.

Josie looked after her down the hall. "That's all *right*," she mocked. Zabrina laughed as she looked at Amy, who smiled awkwardly.

"Did you see the way Luke was looking at her when she was debating?" Zabrina asked Josie as they started down the hall.

"He was looking at her?!" Josie all but snarled, looking back in Grace's direction. "She makes me sick."

SIX
NO PRESSURE

"The best film ever? *Lawrence of Arabia*—epic masterpiece," John Livingston parried.

They were in the teachers' lounge for lunch once again. Bridgett Stevens was in her usual place on the arm of the couch, strumming her guitar.

Zach Brady shook his head. "Old-school. Not a chance, John! *The Shawshank Redemption*'s a much better film. Stronger script, better acting—and the ending!"

John wasn't backing down. "I can't believe we're having this conversation. *Lawrence of Arabia* was nominated for ten Academy Awards and won seven, including Best Picture. How many Oscars did *The Shawshank Redemption* win?"

Zach shrugged.

"Zero. Nada. Zilch. Less than one."

Bridgett stopped playing. "You guys are pathetic. They're both bush league compared to . . ." She let the sentence hang, drawing their attention to a crescendo. "*The Godfather*."

John smiled, "Marlon Brando's opening monologue . . ."

Zach cut in doing his best Brando: "'You don't even think to call me Godfather . . .'"

John tried to top him. "'Instead you come into my house the day my daughter is to be married . . .'"

"'And you ask me to murder,'" Zach finished.

"The music!"

"The costumes!"

"The violence!"

Now it was Bridgett's turn to shake her head. "I'm kidding. I'm kidding."

Both men shot her a perplexed look.

"What film, then?" John asked.

Bridgett looked from John to Zach and back, again pausing for dramatic effect. "*Casablanca*! *Casablanca*!"

Zach's eyes narrowed. "You're not serious."

She mimicked their earlier quips about *The Godfather*. "Black and white, romance . . ."

Livingston shook his head in disbelief.

"Humphrey Bogart, Ingrid Bergman, romance . . ." she went on.

Zach made a gagging face.

"Forbidden love, *romance* . . ." she continued.

"Cigarettes, lung cancer, death," Zach echoed.

"Yeah, whatever." John decided to change the subject. "Have you met, ah, that new student from California, Grácia Davis?"

Zach thought about it for a moment. "I don't think so."

"Well, sure you did," Bridgett countered. "I introduced you two on the first day of school." She looked back at John. "She's very pretty," she added.

"And smart," John countered. "But there's something else too. I can't quite put my finger on it yet, but she's different."

"What's different about her?"

"She's intriguing. Tremendous communicator. All my students love—well, most of my students—love her. She's popular, charismatic, um . . ." He scratched his chin. "But there's something else too."

"Yeah?" Bridgett queried.

"Not sure, but she is different."

"Different good or different bad?" Zach asked.

"That, my friend"—John rapped his knuckles the table—"is the $64,000 question."

"Okay, well, when you find out let me know."

The bell rang, and Zach rose to leave.

John nodded. Bridgett picked up her guitar and started strumming again. John listened for a moment. "That's nice. When's your show again?"

"Next Wednesday, eight o'clock, at the Red Rock Café."

"I'll be there with Brady if I can drag him out on a school night!" He looked at Zach and winked.

Zach shook his head, smiled, and turned to go to class.

* * * * *

Chase approached Mr. B's classroom apprehensively. It was after school and most people were making their way to practice or home for the day. Chase had a few minutes before he had to be at cross country. He wanted to ask Mr. Brady about something, but at the same time, he didn't. Mr. Brady was grading papers with his door open. He caught a glimpse of Chase as he peeked in.

"Chase! I was thinking about you earlier today."

Chase hesitated, stepping up to the threshold. "Hey, Mr. B, you got a minute?"

"Yeah, sure. Come in."

Chase found a desk near the middle of the room to sit in, and Mr. Brady pulled a desk over from nearby and leaned back against it.

"So, what's up? Did you have questions about the Bill of Rights assignment?"

"Um, no," Chase answered, then fell silent.

Mr. Brady waited a beat. "Was it something else then?"

Chase gave an awkward smile. "Yeah."

Another uncomfortable beat.

Mr. Brady looked at the ground and then back to Chase. "I don't mean to pry, Chase, but you seem a little preoccupied these days."

Chase paused again, searching for the right words. "Mr. B . . . have you ever . . . fantasized about a girl?"

Mr. Brady raised his eyebrows and suppressed a laugh. "Excuse me, Chase?"

"No, no, that's, that's not what I meant." Chase tried to reframe his thoughts. "What I meant to say is, I can't stop thinking about . . . There's this girl. She's in my advanced debate class. She's—uh, I don't know—she's just . . ."

Mr. Brady nodded without interrupting.

"She's beautiful, she's smart—and she has this . . . great smile."

Mr. Brady smiled. "And?"

"Well," Chase paused again, "I'm thinking about, um, asking her out." For the first time he looked up at Mr. Brady's face. "So what do you think? Should I, you know . . . I mean—"

Mr. Brady smiled and shook his head. "Have you thought about getting to know her?"

Chase looked as if he'd just asked him what the quadratic equation was.

"You know, talked with her one on one. Why don't you ask her out for coffee? Then there's no pressure."

Chase sighed. "Yeah," he said, talking to himself and nodding. "No pressure." He looked up. "Thanks, Mr. B!" He stood up and gave Mr. Brady a side-five.

"You're welcome, Chase." Mr. Brady smiled. "Just make a friend." He slapped Chase on the shoulder. "You know how to do that, don't you?"

"Yeah," Chase said, talking to himself again. "Make a friend." He slapped Mr. B on the arm, grinning broadly and making for the door. "Thanks again, Mr. B! Have a great weekend!"

* * * * *

Amy saw Chase come out of Mr. B's room as she hurried toward volleyball practice, her books folded in her arms against her chest. As usual, though, he didn't seem to see her.

Amy sighed and slowed her pace. She knew it would make her late, but she didn't care. She could run a couple of laps alone while the rest of the players did drills and chattered about their day—while Grace was the center of attention, again.

She liked being at volleyball practice, though. While it still thrilled her to have Josie and Zabrina bring her in as a friend, she'd been a loner most of the time since middle school—especially since Bobbi started hanging out with Jesse all the time. For some reason it was nice to be at volleyball practice and just be her invisible self again.

She wondered again at how quickly Grace had made friends on the team. She found it hard not to like Grace, though Josie demanded that she did. Grace and Josie were so different, but so much alike. They were both strong and confident, both seemed to have the attention of every person in the room, and were both smart *and* pretty.

But there was a difference too. All of the attention Grace got came naturally, almost accidentally, while Josie demanded it of everyone she met. Though all the guys had noticed her, Grace didn't seem to pay attention to any of them and dated no one. Josie paid attention to all of them—more to the cute ones, of course—and dated *everyone*, but never dated any one guy for very long. It seemed more like a game to her than really getting to know them. In fact, as Amy thought about it, Josie acted as if she never wanted anyone to get to know her at all.

Amy could only wonder what it would be to have boys after her like that. At least when she was with Josie and Zabrina, boys paid attention to her—though it was obvious most of them were interested in Josie first, Zabrina second, and her as the consolation prize. They didn't seem to mind so much, though, if she just went along with what they wanted to do.

A slight chill of fall weather ran down her spine.

At least when they were all three together, Josie broke the party up before anything too uncomfortable happened. Amy imagined being with a boy who was only really interested in who she was, and not what he could convince her to do. She wondered if that were even possible.

As Chase headed into the gym, Amy picked up her pace to follow. She knew he was headed to the track, but he would probably show up at the gym door again on his way out. She wanted to be on the floor when that happened—though she was pretty sure she wasn't the one he was watching for every time he peeked in.

She stifled a frown and broke into a jog.

* * * * *

No pressure, Chase thought. *No pressure.*

He lay on his bed with his feet on his pillow and his head hanging over the edge. He looked at his room upside down in the mirror. He was clutching his iPhone, and Grace's number was dialed into it—but he had yet to press the call button.

He dropped his headphones around his neck and raised the phone to his ear, finger approaching the call button now. He took a deep breath. Then he sighed, sat up, and took the phone away from his head.

Another sigh.

No pressure, he thought. *Right. As if.*

He needed a different approach.

He spun off of his bed and landed with a thump on the floor, leaning against its footboard.

Another sigh. A big one.

He stood up and looked in the mirror, squinting his eyes like Clint Eastwood in *Dirty Harry. Mr. B's right. Don't be a coward, Chase.*

Without giving it a second thought, he pressed call and put the phone to his ear.

One ring.

He panicked at the sound and hung up.

"No! NO!" He picked up a pillow and screamed into it. Several times.

You idiot! She's gonna see your number!

He knew he needed to call back before she did. Now what?

Simple. *Confidence music—brilliant!* He put his headphones back on and started bouncing to his favorite song: "Remember that Rhyme."

Bouncing. Dancing. More bouncing. A few jumping jacks. Some fist push-ups. Air guitar. Clap push-ups. More bouncing.

He dialed again and pushed "call." It was ringing.

When the line picked up, trying to sound as cool as he could, he said, "Hi, this is Chase, Chase Morgan. How are you?"

"I'm fine," OB answered, speaking rather deliberately as if confused. "What's wrong with your voice?"

Chase jumped and rolled his eyes. He cleared his throat loudly. "Ah, nothing, sorry." He took a breath to slow his heartbeat. "OB, I need your advice."

"G'ahead. I'm listening."

"I . . . ah . . . tried calling Grace tonight."

"Let me guess," OB cut in. "You hung up after one ring?"

"How'd you know?"

OB shook his head. "It happens to all of us, bro."

"Really?"

OB nodded, even though Chase couldn't see it.

"So what should I do?"

OB spoke in his most OB-Wan-like voice. "Well, the way I see it, you have two choices, my son."

Chance hung on every word, but OB was waiting to be asked. "I'm listening," Chase prompted.

OB tried to sound like a football coach during a halftime pep talk. "One: You can get back on that phone and dial until she answers . . ."

Again a pause. "Or?" Chase prompted again.

"You can quit trying and be tormented by thoughts of 'What if?' for the rest of your life . . . life . . ." He let his voice trail off and counted to three before echoing one more, "Life . . ."

Chase was annoyed by the dramatics and didn't like either alternative, but none of that mattered. "Seriously, OB, what would you do?"

"That's easy. *I*," he emphasized, "would quit trying."

"Really?"

"It beats rejection, my dude. Believe me, it beats rejec—" He stopped midsentence. "Hey, uh, is that 4 Days in Geneva in the background?"

"Yup."

"Confidence music, huh?"

"You know it."

Chase's phone buzzed. He had another call. He looked to see who it was. "Ahhh!"

"Chase, what's—what's wrong?!"

"Nothin'! Um, uh . . . there's a spider—giant spider—freaking me out. I gotta go kill it. I'll call you back later."

"Dude! *Dude!*"

Chase hung up.

He looked himself squarely in the eyes again in the mirror. *It's time, punk.*

He pressed answer. The call clicked through and he froze, breathing heavily.

"Hello?" Grace's voice came through the phone. "*He-llll-oooo!*"

Chase sounded like Darth Vader.

She paused. "I can hear you breathing—*heavily.*"

"Hello?" Chase tried to sound surprised. His voice cracked a little.

"Chase?" Grace said. "Is this you?"

"Uh huh."

"You called?"

"I did?"

"Yeah. Yeah, you did. Your number popped up on my phone. Did you need something?"

"Uh," he paused, turning the phone away from his mouth. "Gosh, this is hard."

"What did you just say?" Grace sounded surprised.

"Um . . ." Chase drew out.

"Did you just say, 'Gosh'?"

"Maybe."

Grace took the phone in her other hand and sat up. "Why didn't you just say 'God'?"

Chase was lost. "I dunno. When I was little . . ." He stopped dead in his tracks.

Silence.

"I'm listening," Grace prompted.

"You know, we were taught that . . ." He took a big breath. "This is so lame."

Grace smiled, suppressing a giggle. "Go on."

"Well, you know, when I was little I was taught that saying 'God' in that way is, like— like, taking God's name in vain."

"Chase?" Grace's voice was serious now.

"Yeah?"

"Are you a Christian?"

"Um . . ." Chase froze again. He didn't know what to say. If he said yes and she wasn't a Christian, she might be turned off—but if he said no, he'd be lying. On the other hand, if she *was* a Christian, she might find out somehow that he was being dishonest and she'd think he was a coward. He had to say something and quick.

"Um . . ." He paused again. "Well . . . no."

"You're not?" Her voice sank.

He corrected himself. "No, no, um—no. I'm sorry. What I meant to say is, no-o-o . . ." He drew the word out. "No-o-body's really ever asked me that before."

Another uncomfortable beat.

"So . . . you *are* a Christian?"

"Yes . . . but I'm not, like, a fanatic—or, you know, anything like that!"

Grace said nothing for what seemed too long. *A total turnoff*, he thought.

He tried to cover it up. "Guess I'll just see you at school on Monday."

He was ready to hang up when Grace said, "This is amazing."

Chase was sure he'd heard that wrong. "It is?"

"Yeah." There was a smile in her voice—he could see it. "I've been praying for a Christian friend. You called completely out of the blue. Chase, you're the answer to my prayers."

"I am?" This was not at all the way he had seen this conversation going.

Again, the smile in her voice. "I might be too forward, but, um . . . do you wanna meet up?"

"Me? Now? Like, right now?"

"I'm being too forward . . ."

"No," Chase assured her. "No, not at all. Um. . . no, it's, ah, cool."

"Okay, so, what do you say? Raising Cane's in twenty minutes? My treat?"

"Uh, yeah. Yeah. Yeah sure."

"Bye, Chase." The words came short and crisp. There was a lightness in them, almost a bounce, like someone skipping.

Chase fell back on his bed as if he was falling into a swimming pool. He took a deep breath, looked at his iPhone for a minute in disbelief, then dialed as if something had just occurred to him.

"'Ello, Guv'nah," OB answered in a Cockney accent.

"Are you sitting down?"

"Yes." OB answered him like it was a stupid question, then, with concern, said, "Was that spider poisonous?"

Chase had completely forgotten about the made-up spider. "No. I'm fine."

"Then what's the problem?"

"I, uh . . . I called Grace."

"I told you not to call, my dude. Torment is definitely better than rejection."

"OB." Chase gave it a beat. "She didn't reject me."

"Say *what?*"

"Except for now I have a serious problem."

"What's that?" OB still couldn't believe what he was hearing.

"She wants to go out. *Now!*"

"Whoa! Whoa, whoa, whoa, whoa, whoa—*whoa!* Don't take this personally, my dude, but why does she want to go out with *you?*"

Chase shrugged. "She thinks I'm an answer to prayer." He spoke as if he didn't believe it either.

"So," OB deduced, "she's nuts?"

"No, no, I don't think so." He was trying to talk himself into it as well. "She's a Christian, and she's been praying for a Christian friend, and . . . I happened to call."

"Man! Why can't I get that lucky?" He spoke as if reading a classified ad. "'Desperate, beautiful Christian girl wants *a friend*.' It's too easy!" OB paused thinking about it. "So, how did she know you were a Christian?"

"I said, 'Gosh.'"

"Say, *what*?"

Chase shook his head. "It's a long story, but, um . . . dude, I only have seventeen minutes 'til I have to meet her. I gotta go get ready."

"Dude!"

"I know! Later."

"Dude! Dude!"

Chase hung up and popped up off of his bed to go get ready. He felt like he was flying.

SEVEN
HOW DO YOU TALK TO A PRETTY GIRL?

Jesse Valentine and his mother lived in a two-bedroom loft apartment in the Thibault Towers Luxury Apartment Complex. Jesse knew the pool and the workout facilities there all too well. Most of the inhabitants were wealthy older couples, young up-and-comer couples who had yet to have kids, or singles. Jesse spent a lot of time working out with bachelors or twentysomething women who thought he was cute but never really paid much attention to him. Sometimes they would flirt with him a little, then ignore him when a young doctor or lawyer came in to use the treadmill or free weights. It was a strange kind of lonely for him.

Friday nights were always dead in the gym, though, so he sat in their apartment with a plate of crumbs from a bologna sandwich he had just made himself. It was after 8:00 p.m. when his mom finally came through the door—on the cell phone, as usual. "If I'd have had any idea how complicated that case was, I never would have agreed to it!"

She took her keys out of the door and put her things down on the kitchen counter. She looked around inspecting the apartment. It was spotless. Then she circled out to come into the living room, where Jesse sat staring at a television he'd been too bored to turn on.

"It goes to arbitration Monday morning!" She listened to the person on the other side of the phone and then laughed. "Okay, sure, ten a.m. sharp! See ya there!" She hung up.

"Hey, Mom," Jesse said without looking up. "How was work?"

She collapsed into a chair. "Busy!" She exhaled, then smiled. "I see you found something to eat! Good for you."

Jesse had learned long ago it wasn't worth waiting for his mom to come home so she could pull out cold leftovers from a business luncheon and try to convince him it was better than homemade. Some nights she didn't even come home before he went to bed. He wasn't much of a cook, but he could make a sandwich or a box of Kraft macaroni and cheese. She always acted as if it was a big adult thing when he did it, but she didn't fool him.

He shrugged.

"So, how was school?" His mom was in a good mood. Though she'd been complaining about it for the last week, Jesse guessed the case she was working on was getting her some attention at work. She always seemed perkier when the partners gave her a case they saw as "a chance to prove herself." Jesse knew that just meant she would be more distracted than ever, but his mom thrived on it. Even when she was home, all she did was work. Even on Friday nights.

"I dunno," he said dully, looking at the painting his mom had bought at some art exhibit where people talked in little groups and drank expensive wine. "School's school." She had only been home a few minutes, and he already wanted to leave. He wanted to get out before she buried herself in her laptop. "Um, is it cool if I hang out with Bobbi tonight?"

"That would be great. I am swamped."

No surprise, Jesse thought.

"How's she doing?"

For the first time, Jesse looked right at her. His brow furrowed. "I don't know, why?"

His mom pursed her lips, thinking. "She just seems . . ." She got up to go to the kitchen, taking down a wineglass. "I don't know—sad lately."

Jesse was a little surprised his mom had noticed how someone else felt. "I haven't noticed anything, but . . ." He shrugged again.

His phone vibrated on the coffee table. He picked it up and looked at it. "Speaking of Bobbi." He showed the display to his mom so she could see Bobbi had just texted.

She smiled and looked at Jesse. Looking into his eyes, her face clouded.

"What?"

She shook it off and lowered her eyes. "You look more like your father every day," she said.

Jesse broke eye contact. He didn't like talking about his father, especially with his mom. She was never honest about him. She always said good things about him, but if that were the case, why had he left? Why did he find a girlfriend and move away? Why didn't he ever call?

Jesse texted Bobbi a reply. "I'll be home by one," he said, jumping up to kiss his mother on the cheek. He walked out the door without looking back.

She sat staring into the living room where Jesse had just been, listening until the door shut behind him.

"Be good to her, Jesse," she said softly. Her voice shook a little.

* * * * *

Chase pulled his jeep into an empty parking spot in front of Raising Cane's Chicken Fingers. He'd earned enough working at the hardware store the summer before his junior year to buy the jeep, and he'd been fixing it up a little here and there ever since. Just before the summer was over he and his dad had painted it a deep blue. The last addition was a sticker they had pasted upside down and across the top of the windshield that read, "If you can read this, PULL ME OUT!" His dad thought it was hilarious. His mom, not so much.

He looked into the restaurant and saw Grace sitting in a booth watching for him through the window. She waved and smiled. He waved back sheepishly and turned to jump out. His seat belt snapped him back into place. He felt Grace laughing, but didn't look.

I don't think I can do this.

Cool Chase scoffed. *Listen, punk, you've come this far. There's no turning back.*

He unsnapped the seat belt and climbed out. He pulled a Tic Tac° box out of his pocket and took a swig, then circled his car the long way to avoid looking back through the window at Grace.

He made his way inside, ordered at the counter, and went to sit with Grace.

"Hey!" she said.

"Hi!" He sat down.

"So . . ." She smiled.

"So?"

"What's new?" Grace prompted.

Chase shrugged. "Not much."

Grace tried again. "How was your week?"

"It was . . . pretty good."

"Enjoying debate?"

Chase winced slightly. "I mean, sort of."

Grace fought rolling her eyes.

The food arrived, and they thanked the waitress.

Grace smiled, being friendly. "So are we gonna . . . do this all night?"

"Hmm?" Chase asked, cluelessly.

She looked at him somewhat pleadingly. "I was hoping we'd have a conversation."

Chase dropped his eyes. "Uh, sorry." He took a deep breath. "I'm not very experienced at this."

"At what?"

"*Dating*?" he offered sheepishly.

Grace's breath caught in her throat. "You think this is a 'date'?"

Chase shrugged. "Kind of."

"Really?" Grace almost laughed.

"What is it then? I mean—" Chase was out of his depths again.

"I don't know," Grace answered. "Two friends . . . eating chicken fingers . . . getting to know each other?"

No pressure. Mr. B's words echoed in Chase's mind. He dropped his eyes again, not sure how to recover. He'd assumed too much. *OB was right. It's better to not try than—*

"Chase?" Grace's voice broke his reverie.

He looked up.

"Can we start over?"

Chase shook his head, not understanding. His eyes narrowed.

"I want you to think of me as . . . a friend . . . you haven't met yet."

Chase's whole body relaxed. He smiled. "Yeah, yeah. I can do that."

Grace reached her hand across the table. "Hi, I'm Grácia Davis." Chase took her hand to shake it. "Please, call me Grace." And there it was again, that smile.

Chase let all the pretense fall away. "I love your name, Grácia!" He paused. "How'd you get it?"

"My mom," she answered softly. "She had three miscarriages before I came along, and . . . the doctors . . . they told her she'd never be able to have kids. So, she knew it was only by God's 'amazing grace' that I was born."

"Hmm. That's beautiful." Chase had been impressed with Grace's natural beauty, but now he was finding out there was more to her than he'd imagined. "Okay . . . I'm Chase Morgan, but you can call me . . ." He thought for a moment, then just said, "Um, Chase."

Grace smiled broadly. She knew Chase was starting to relax, and she appreciated a good sense of humor. "So," she asked. "How long have you lived here?"

"My whole life."

Her eyes widened. "Seriously?"

"Yup."

"Wow! I've never met anyone who's lived their entire life in the same town before."

Chase smiled. "Not just same town—same block, same house, same bedroom, same neighbors, same friends, same

Spiderman underwear." Chase looked to see the expression on her face. "I'm just kidding."

Grace's laugh jingled again.

"Our neighbors moved away a year ago."

Grace's laughter exploded this time, and she almost coughed up a French fry.

Chase laughed with her.

"What about you? Where have you lived?"

Grace took a sip of her drink. "Where *haven't* I lived?!" She shrugged. "I was born in Florida, we moved to Massachusetts when I was two. When I was five we moved to Phoenix . . ."

At the moment, Chase realized he wasn't nervous anymore. He just smiled and rode along on the cadence of Grace's voice.

* * * * *

Jesse pulled his old football out of the trunk of his car and jogged toward where he saw Bobbi sitting on the bleachers. It was Friday night, and Eastglenn had played a tight game the night before against McKinley—barely winning, 21-20. It was one of their few Thursday night games. McKinley had scored with seconds left and decided to go for two, but Cisco Diaz jumped the route on the pass and saved the game. Eastglenn hadn't beaten McKinley in seven years.

As was tradition, the night after a win, Eastglenn left the lights on at the field for local kids to come and re-enact the glory of the night before. Most nights now, though, since the advent of the Xbox and PlayStation, the stadium was usually empty. Plus, since Eastglenn won so seldom, people had kind of forgotten the tradition. Even as public as the field was, it was an easy place to meet for anyone who wanted to get away from the crowd and be on their own.

It was a place filled with a lot of mixed memories for Jesse. As a sophomore, he'd been a promising QB prospect and got brought up to varsity to be backup when two of their three QBs went down in consecutive weeks. A couple weeks later, when Eastglenn's third consecutive losing season was assured, Jesse was put in when the previous third-stringer was struggling. Jesse threw two touchdown passes in the fourth quarter to put a scare into Belaire, who won 31-28 when Jesse's last pass of the evening went right through the arms of his receiver into the awaiting hands of the free safety. People were talking about him as the potential starter for the next season.

Soon after, his dad had moved to California with his twentysomething girlfriend. Even though separated already, his mom and dad had been fighting a lot and found it hard to be in the vicinity of one another. It didn't help that his dad was a football enthusiast and his mom hated the game. She just knew it would permanently cripple Jesse at some point. Suddenly without his dad's support, his mom's constant barrage against the game began to wear on Jesse. It was weird too. She had a lot to say about football, but they never once talked about his dad leaving. She'd just buried herself all the more in trying to make partner.

In the second half of his sophomore year, Jesse's grades dropped and he got into an argument with one of the coaches during spring practice. Had it not been for Bobbi's help in math, he could have flunked out. Jesse's mother insisted he quit the team after the argument with his coach. She went to the principal and said the coach had been abusive, then threatened legal action against the district. In the end, Jesse decided he was done with football—and his mom left it at that.

Whenever Jesse met Bobbi at the field, memories of that last game usually came along, as well as memories of his dad and the fact that he hadn't spoken to him in months. Football was the glue in his relationship with his father, and now that he wasn't playing and his dad lived in California, there was no reason for them to stay in touch. Bobbi was always his best distraction from all of that.

As Bobbi trotted onto the field, Jesse lofted a perfect spiral toward her. When she caught sight of the ball, Bobbi gave out a high-pitched squeal and ran out of the way. The ball bounced harmlessly across the turf and under a bench.

Jesse laughed. Bobbi was wearing those tight, tattered blue jeans he liked so much. Even when she was running scared, they showed her figure off well. He felt a thrill of excitement just looking at her.

"I'm not sure you're cut out for this game," he said.

Bobbi spun around, fished the ball out from under the bench, and came running at him. "That's what you think!" She made a couple moves as if she were going for a touchdown if

Jesse didn't do something—so he ran out, grabbed her around the waist, lifted her into the air, and spun her gently to the ground. She rolled onto her back and looked straight into his eyes. He was lost for a moment. As he leaned in to kiss her, she thrust the ball into his chest and rolled out from beneath him. "Hit me on a post!" she called out, running for the sideline.

Jesse laughed. He tried to float one to her soft enough to catch.

For the next half hour or so, they ran around the football field playing catch, laughing, and tumbling in the grass. Even when she was awkward, Jesse loved the way she moved. Each tackle was a bit gentler, and each time he tried to hold her a little bit longer.

Eventually, though, she tired of the game and the roughhousing, and they went to sit in the bleachers. Jesse lay along one of the bleachers with his head in Bobbi's lap, looking up into the sky.

"So, see those three stars in a row there?" Jesse pointed.

Bobbi squinted against the stadium lights. "The ones that look like they're kind of in the middle of an hourglass?"

"Yeah, right," Jesse said. "The three stars are called Orion's Belt, and the hourglass shape is Orion himself."

Bobbi squinted again to see it. "He must have broad shoulders."

Jesse laughed. "Yeah. And thick legs."

They both laughed and then fell silent, staring up at the sky.

"So what are we doing?"

Jesse looked up into her eyes. "We're looking at the stars, babe."

Bobbi shook her head and looked out at the field. "That's not what I mean."

"What do you mean?"

"Where is *this* going?"

"This?"

Bobbi pointed to Jesse and then herself.

"You and me?"

"Yeah."

Jesse looked up at the stars again and shrugged. "I don't know."

"Well, what do you mean *you don't know*?" Bobbi asked impatiently.

"I mean, I don't know. I'm having fun," Jesse said. "Aren't you having fun?"

"Yeah, yeah, of course," Bobbi agreed. "Just . . . fun's not everything."

"Well . . . okay," Jesse agreed. "But it's good for now. Isn't now"—he pointed to her and then back to himself—"good?"

Bobbi shook her head. "Yeah, but where do you see us in the future? Where are we going?"

Jesse looked back into the sky, avoiding eye contact. After an awkward silence, he pointed up again. "See that, right there?"

Bobbi looked up too. "Yeah."

"Pegasus."

Bobbi's eyes fell back on Jesse. She wasn't smiling anymore. "What?"

He pointed again, and Bobbi looked up again. "I mean, it's upside down, but that's the head." He traced the outline with his finger. "And that's the neck, and then the front legs there. Pretty cool, hey?"

Bobbi looked off at the field again. "Jesse, I don't care about Pegasus. I asked you a serious question."

Jesse lost his patience. "I don't know, okay? I don't know!" he said defensively. "I don't think, like, I don't think about it."

"Well, what *do* you think about, Jess?" There was accusation in her voice.

He shook his head, looking back at the stars. "Stuff."

Bobbi saw the hurt on his face—hurt that was hard for him to express. It was one of the things that drew her to him. Though he never admitted it, she knew he needed her, and that felt good. Sometimes he just seemed like a little kid who needed to be held and kissed.

Jesse looked back up into Bobbi's eyes. He saw the look of affection and vulnerability. "So . . ." he said softly, "wanna go for a drive?"

Bobbi didn't know what he was really asking. "Right now?" she said. She had a picture in her mind of them kissing earlier and rolling around on the football field, but she wasn't sure why.

He nodded, that big silly grin on his face again.

EIGHT
LATER THAT NIGHT

When they had finished eating and talking, Chase felt unusually content. He'd never been so comfortable speaking with a girl before. At the same time, he had to admit he'd never really talked to many he wasn't related to. Sure, he'd gone out with girls to dances and stuff, but he usually double-dated with OB, and OB did enough talking for the both of them. This was something different—something totally different—and it was a "different" he liked. *No pressure,* he thought again. *Thanks, Mr. B.*

Grace's mom had given her a ride into town, so Grace asked if she could get a ride home. Chase was glad to have extra time to talk some more, though as it turned out, they exchanged more smiles than words. It wasn't always so easy to carry on a conversation in his jeep when the top was off, anyway—but he didn't feel as if they needed chatter to fill the air between them.

Grace's house was next to a small lake that had an island in it. A previous owner had built a bridge to the island and a tree house in the stand of trees just on the island side. There was even a little fire pit. Since the Davises had moved around so much, they had gotten good at finding great properties that they could rent. This, however, was the first house they'd actually purchased. Dr. Davis had done his doctoral work at LSU, and both he and Mrs. Davis vowed they'd settle down in Louisiana someday—and that day had come. They finally had their dream home in Baton Rouge.

For some reason, when Chase heard they'd bought the house, he was glad.

Grace asked hesitantly, "Do you wanna . . . come in and meet my family?"

"Really?"

Grace nodded and smiled.

Chase nodded back.

They got out of the jeep and went into the house.

As Grace opened the front door, they heard, "Gracie! Come bring your new friend and have a bite to eat. Your father just made his world-famous nachos." Salsa music was blaring from the back of the house.

Chase looked at her. "*Gracie?*" Then after a beat, "And how did she know someone was with you?"

Grace rolled her eyes, shrugged, and gave a weak smile. "Moms," was all she offered.

They followed the music into the kitchen. A preteen boy with the same skin coloring as Grace sat with a girl in pigtails and freckles on stools at the kitchen island. Grace's dad broke off sections of a huge tray of nachos onto smaller plates. Mrs. Davis was already out from behind the island on the way to greet them.

She said something to Chase, but he indicated he didn't hear it over the music.

She turned back to the others. "Jonah! Turn the music down!"

"Mom!" the boy answered.

"Now!"

He jumped off of his stool and went to the stereo to turn it down, but not very much. Mrs. Davis shot him a stern look. He threw up his hands in disbelief, then turned it down more.

"You must be Chase Morgan," Grace's mom said again. "I've heard a lot about you." She gave Chase a big hug that caught him by surprise. She all but winked at Grace. "So, you're in Mr. Livingston's debate class together. I hear he's an interesting teacher. Gracie tells me you've been stalking her."

Grace seemed shocked. "Mom!"

Mrs. Davis gave her a smirk filled with mischief. "I'm kidding! I'm kidding! I think it's cute that Chase is watching over you."

Grace glared at her, but her mom only giggled. She turned to the others to make introductions. "Anywho, this is Gracie's little brother, Jonah."

He came up and offered Chase his hand. "Hey, bro, wassup?" After they shook, Jonah gave him a hug too. Again, Chase went a little stiff.

"And this is our neighbor and Jonah's 'good friend.'" Mrs. Davis winked at Chase. "Meet Hannah Banana."

"Mom!" Jonah said. "I saw that."

"Take a chill pill!" she scolded affectionately. Then, conspiratorially to Chase, she added, "But don't they look cute together?"

Not being able to hear them over the music, Hannah smiled and waved.

Mr. Davis cleared his throat loudly. Obviously he didn't want to be left out.

"Oh!" Mrs. Davis said. "And the hunk over here—making all of these nachos—he's my personal chef, Dr. *Caliente* Davis."

Grace's dad came over, took off his oven mitts, and shook Chase's hand. Chase braced for another hug, but Dr. Davis just smiled. "How ya doing, son? You can call me *Dr*. Davis," he said in a deep voice. Then he slapped him on the arm. "Just kidding. My name's Andrew." He indicated the plates on the island. "Can I get you some nachos?"

"Uh, sure. Not a lot, though. We just ate."

"Coming right up." Dr. Davis filled a plate with nachos to overflowing, put it in front of one of the stools, and indicated to Chase the place was his.

What followed was something beyond anything Chase had ever experienced. Grácia's family had a kinetic energy unlike any family he had ever met. They were smart and affectionate, and anything but shy about showing either quality. After quipping around the table for about a half hour and eating nachos, the music came back up, the furniture was pushed back, and Chase was treated to a salsa lesson initiated by Jonah. Jonah and Hannah, Dr. and Mrs. Davis, and Chase and Grace danced into the night.

* * * * *

Jesse had driven to the Tracks, a place familiar to everyone at Eastglenn. It was a secluded spot just north of town. The coyotes were in full chorus as Jesse turned on the radio. He pulled Bobbi close and they began kissing. After a few minutes, when his hands began to wander, Bobbi pushed him away and looked out the passenger-side window.

Bobbi whispered under her breath, "Oh God, what am I doing?"

Jesse slumped back into the driver's seat and slammed his foot down in frustration.

She looked up. "Please help me."

Jesse collected himself. "Bobbi," he said softly. He snuggled his face into her shoulder. "Bobbi, I don't . . . babe, I don't want you to feel any pressure. I just want you to know that I . . ." He looked up at her. "I love you."

They sat quietly for a moment, Jesse's head resting on her shoulder. Bobbi stared out the window, and a small tear trickled down her cheek. She wiped it away.

Jesse pulled away, frustrated, caressing her shoulder with one hand.

Bobbi turned to look at him. *He does love me,* she thought. She let his words sink in.

She turned in her seat to look at him.

He turned and looked at her sadly.

She allowed herself a half smile, then inched toward him. She studied her hands for a moment, then looked up into his eyes. Big blue eyes.

He loves me. A warm grin spread across her face. Her face lit up gradually from brooding to a full smile.

Holding his face cradled in her hands, she pulled his face toward hers.

* * * * *

The dancing at the Davises' didn't stop until Dr. Davis threw up his hands and said he was too tired to go on. He and his wife retired to the front room to read, and Jonah, Hannah, Grace, and Chase went outside to sit on the porch and talk. Jonah was still too wired to just chat, though, so he pestered Grace until she agreed to sing with him. Hannah and Chase were treated to an impromptu a cappella concert that included "Amazing Grace," "Lean on Me," and "House of the Rising Sun."

After "Rising Sun," they heard Hannah's dad call from next door: "Hannah! Time to come home."

She looked at all of them apologetically. "I have to go."

Grace wrapped her arm around her for a side hug. "Bye, Hannah Banana."

"Bye, Gracie." She held her hand out to Chase. "Nice meeting you, Chase."

Chase shook it. "You too, Hannah."

Hannah started walking toward her house.

"Hey, what about me?" Jonah pointed at himself.

Hannah turned back toward the three of them. "See *you* tomorrow."

Jonah sat back smugly. "That's better, girlfriend."

Hannah put her hands on her hips. "In your dreams!" she said with attitude, then turned back toward home.

When she was out of earshot, Grace mussed her brother's hair. "Shut *down*!"

Jonah pushed her away and recombed his hair with his fingers. Chase and Grace laughed.

Jonah, regaining his composure, put his hand on Chase's shoulder. "So kids, what are we going to do now?"

"Mmm," Grace pondered. "*You*—are going to go *inside*—and read a very long book."

Jonah popped up and did a few more salsa moves. "Ah, come on, Gracie! The night is young! We just got this party started!"

His sister was having none of it.

He turned to Chase. "Work with me, Chase?" He bumped him with his shoulder, dancing again.

Chase looked at Grace, then back at Jonah. He shrugged and pointed to Grace. "Uhh . . ."

"Chase!" Jonah pleaded. There was no hope. "Okay, I'm going, I'm going," Jonah surrendered. "Peace out." He thumped his fist to his chest and then pointed a peace sign to Chase and Grace. Chase responded in kind.

As soon as Jonah was in the house, Grace leaned over to Chase and whispered, "He really likes you!"

They both laughed. Grace scooted over closer to Chase, cutting the space between them in half.

"Whatcha thinkin'?" she asked, leaning toward him again.

Chased raised his hands in disbelief. "Your family!"

Grace looked at the ground. "Pretty crazy, huh?" she said noncommittally. She knew they could be a lot to take in at once.

"No," Chase said, "they're, sincere, spontaneous, fun . . ." He looked at her. "Just like you."

Grace gave him a sideways smile, then looked back toward her feet.

Chase heard the door open behind them. It was Mrs. Davis. She crossed on tiptoes to the table where her book and a half glass of water sat. She picked them up and turned to sneak back into the house. When she saw that Chase had noticed her, she winked and gave him a finger wave, then stole back into the house.

He looked back at Grace, surprise on his face. She chose that moment to look back at him. "What?" she asked.

Chase looked behind them. "Your mom just winked at me."

Grace's mom was just shutting one side of the French doors that opened onto the porch. When she saw that Grace had seen her, she blew a kiss to her from behind the glass and disappeared.

Grace's mouth dropped open, and her cheeks flushed. She dropped her face into her hand, mortified.

Chase laughed, then looked at his iPhone. "I'd better go. I have work in the morning."

Grace looked impressed. "You have a job?"

Chase shrugged it off. "Family business," he responded, as if that made it not count. "We own a hardware store in Monticello."

"Hmm. Nice." Grace smiled again.

They got up and walked to the driveway. Grace stood by the front entrance of the house as Chase circled around the back of his jeep and then climbed in the other side. He looked at Grace, who stood smiling and swaying slightly back and forth.

He waved again. She waved back. He started the jeep, put it into drive, and pulled away, that smile the only thing he could think of.

* * * * *

Jesse pulled his car up in front of Bobbi's house. Bobbi sat staring out the passenger-side window, eyes glazed, fixed on nothing. She seemed to hardly even notice the car had stopped.

Jesse looked at her, not sure what to do. "I had a really good time tonight," he said, trying to reassure her.

Bobbi turned for the first time and looked at him as if she didn't recognize his face. She gave a weak smile with no warmth in it. Jesse leaned over to give her a kiss goodnight.

She spun away from him and out the door.

"Bobbi!" he called after her, almost indignant. He unlatched his seat belt and jumped out the door to follow her. "Bobbi, c'mon! Bobbi! *Bobbi!*"

She stopped but didn't turn around. Her face contorted against breaking into tears. She couldn't look at him.

Jesse looked at the ground and put his hand on the back of his neck. He shook his head. Then he walked slowly toward Bobbi, unsure of what he was going to do. He wanted to tell her it was all right. He wanted to tell her it was not a big deal, that it was normal—but he was also afraid she'd overreact again.

He stepped up behind her and spoke softly. He reached for her shoulder, but decided better at the last instant. "It's just that . . . you didn't say anything on the way home." He dropped his head toward her shoulder, but again stopped before it made contact.

"I'm fine, Jesse," she said. Her voice betrayed the fact that she was anything but fine. She might as well have screamed, "Just leave me alone!" and run into the house.

Jesse gently brushed her hair aside and kissed the side of her neck. "I love you, babe," he whispered gently into her ear. "I'm not just saying that." He held his head against hers.

For a moment, they both stood motionless.

Then Bobbi's face twisted again. She pulled away from him and ran into the house, slamming the door behind her.

Jesse stared after her, looking at the closed door. His mouth hung slightly open in confusion. He couldn't really focus.

The night was silent except for a few crickets and the occasional sound of a dog barking from a few blocks away. He waited for Bobbi to run back out to him and say, "I love you too."

After a few painful moments he realized she wasn't coming back out. He shook his head slightly, responding to an uncomfortable thought. Looking up to the sky, he turned and made his way back toward the car.

* * * * *

When Chase got home, he found his parents in the kitchen, dipping warm chocolate-chip cookies in milk, their faces a little too close together for his comfort. A tray still sat on top of the stove, and the mixing bowl still had some dough on it. His mom had flour fingerprints on the side of her face. He couldn't figure out which was gooier: the cookies or the way his parents were looking at each other. He wanted to back out of the room before they realized he was there, but he was too slow.

"Oh!" his mom said, brushing her cheek.

"Uh, hi, Mom, Dad. Have a good night."

"Whoa, whoa, whoa, son, come back here," his dad said without breaking eye contact with his wife. "Tell us about your night." He rolled himself sideways and looked at Chase.

Chase took a big breath and a step back into the kitchen. "What d'ya wanna know?"

"Well, who'd you go out with?" his mom asked.

"A new student."

His dad could tell he was being vague. "Where's he from?"

Chase gave in. "She," he admitted. "California."

His parents looked at each other with raised eyebrows.

"Oh, *she*," his mom said.

"Yeah." Chase wasn't able to keep his face from betraying how much he'd enjoyed the evening. "Her name is Grácia Davis, but she likes being called Grace."

"Oh, Spanish?"

"Actually, Puerto Rican. I think her dad is Irish, though."

"Really?" his mom said. She seemed a little surprised he knew so much about her. "How'd you two meet?"

"Debate," Chase answered.

"Ah," his dad cut in. "Is she pretty?"

"Donald!"

"Ah, sorry!" He cleared his voice. "Uh, is she smart?"

"She's smart," Chase answered. "And gorgeous."

"Y-y-yes!" his dad said, giving him a high-five.

His mom tried to hide her amusement. "Well, do we get to meet Grace?"

"I dunno, we've only really hung out this once."

"Well," his dad cooed, "that's all it took for me to fall in love with this beautiful woman." He took her hand and kissed it. "Remember how we first met?"

She looked at him knowingly. "Quiz meet in Ohio."

"No one could jump at the buzzer like you."

"Oh, Donald!"

"Night!" Chase said, knowing he wanted to be out of there before he saw any more.

"Goodnight, son," his dad called after him. "Love ya!"

"Goodnight, honey," he heard from his mom as he turned up the stairs.

"Don't let the bedbugs bite!" his dad called.

But Chase had already reached the top of the stairs and closed his bedroom door.

* * * * *

Chase felt a strange anticipation when he woke up for school the next Monday morning. He wasn't quite sure why, but getting ready didn't feel as routine as it normally did. He took a little extra time combing his hair and brushing his teeth. He did a little more primping and a lot less flexing and dawdling. He even got to Livingston's class before the first bell rang, just a few seconds before Grace came in and flashed him that beautiful smile of hers. OB slipped in at the very last second and mouthed, "Where were you?" Chase just nodded to him and went back to talking with Grace. OB's brow furrowed, then he smiled and gave Chase a subtle thumbs-up.

Chase soon found he was looking forward to going to debate each morning even though Livingston still scared him a bit. OB realized long before Chase did that it wasn't because he had suddenly become a fan of arguing opinions in front of the class.

As September passed into October, where Grace had drifted between groups at lunch before, she now became a regular sitting with OB and Chase. OB still supplied most of the entertainment for them, but Chase no longer felt he was on the outside looking in. He could smile and laugh at OB's antics with Grace and not feel he was intruding. Grace had an easy confidence and competence about her that Chase admired. While he knew that Grace and OB added something special to their group, he was still not quite sure what his part was. Most of the time he felt himself at a loss for how to join in their bantering and cracking jokes. He found himself nodding and smiling a lot—at least when he wasn't laughing uncontrollably.

Chase was no longer really at a loss for what to do on Friday or Saturday nights anymore either. With OB playing football, Chase and Grace sat together to watch the game when the team was at home. If it was an away game, they usually caught a movie together. OB only rarely came out after the games because he was either too tired or had left too much of himself on the field after they'd lost (which Eastglenn usually did). So Chase either ended up at the Davises' or Grace came over to play games at the Morgans'. Mr. Morgan loved charades, and Mrs. Morgan always wanted Grace on her team so that they would win. Mr.

Davis continued to supply nachos on demand, and Mrs. Davis continued to wink at Chase when he least expected it.

By November, Saturday nights usually meant the three of them were walking around the mall together or hanging out at one of their houses. OB formed a rather solid bond with Mr. Davis's nachos.

With Bobbi's locker not far from Grace's, it didn't take long for Grace to sense that something seemed different about her. Before, Bobbi and Jesse had spent a lot of time there talking nose to nose, but now Bobbi always seemed short with him and had no patience for his advances. One time when this seemed particularly abrupt, Grace and Jesse locked eyes. For once, Grace's warm smile was gone, and Jesse responded with a look that was far from his usual disarming boyish grin.

Grace was slowly becoming concerned about this girl she had yet to actually meet, but she wasn't sure what to do about it. There was something hauntingly familiar about the far-off look in Bobbi's eyes, and Grace knew she needed someone to talk to besides Jesse.

NINE
A COLD DAY IN NOVEMBER

"So, eighty-five percent of youths in prison," Chase argued in front of Mr. Livingston's class, "and seventy-one percent of high-school dropouts all come from single-parent families. While this is far from scientific proof, this statistic strongly suggests that children—especially boys—need the security of a nuclear family to become productive citizens in society. While single parents have the best intentions, it is still strongly suggested that it is best for children if they have both a mother and a father—or at least a strong network of caring adults built around them that help compensate for the absence of those roles—and that there is still an important, if not foundational, place for marriage in society today. Thank you."

Chase sat back down onto the stool next to Grácia, who waited for her turn to speak. The class gave him a polite golf clap. OB shot him a thumbs-up.

"Thank you, Mr. Morgan. Now for the opposition's argument," Mr. Livingston emceed. "Ms. Fullerton, you have the floor."

Josie Fullerton stood and began her argument. "With today's economy, affordable daycare, and a full day of school, women can pursue their dreams with—*or without*—men . . ." Josie presented her arguments with authority, but her audience only paid polite attention, other than maybe a couple of the boys. As far as most of them were concerned, Josie's reputation spoke volumes more than anything she ever said, for better or for worse.

Later, Grace countered, "The decline of marriage is a national crisis. Up until 1970, the percentage of Americans who stayed married never dipped below 93 percent . . ."

Eventually, though, it was Amy who stole the show, making an impassioned and personal argument, telling the story of her aunt who left her husband because she was being abused: "And since then, she has had to raise my three cousins by herself. And the courage and the strength that she has shown in the face of immeasurable pain is . . . It's inspiring. And to say that that's a national crisis that she didn't stay with him, that degrades everything that she's done for them . . ."

When she was done, Mr. Livingston rose to his feet and addressed the class from the back of the room. "Thanks, Josie, Amy, Chase, Grácia—you've got us thinking, and that's a good thing." He paused and looked around. "Thoughts, anyone?"

Cisco raised his hand.

"Cisco?" Mr. Livingston called.

"Every culture evolves, right?"

"Absolutely."

"Well then, maybe the family will be stronger in the long run—you know, with all the changes that are happening."

Grace leaned over to Chase, nudged him, and whispered, "Survival of the fittest."

Mr. Livingston looked Grace's way, having overheard the comment. "Did you hear that, Cisco?" Mr. Livingston pointed toward her. "A little louder, Grácia—so Cisco can hear you."

"I said, 'Survival of the fittest.'"

"And, uh, what did you mean by that?" Mr. Livingston prompted.

"I was referring to Charles Darwin."

"Go on."

"Well, Darwin said in the struggle for survival, the fittest win out at the expense of their rivals, because they adapt better to their environment."

"Yes," Mr. Livingston agreed, "and what does that have to do with what Mr. Diaz is speaking about?"

"I just thought Cisco's statement was a little misleading," Grace countered. "No offense, Cisco."

"None taken," Cisco responded, smiling.

"None taken?" Mr. Livingston choked on the words. "This is debate. Are you going to let her roll you like that?"

Cisco wasn't one to turn away a challenge—especially one thrown down by Mr. Livingston. "Okay, I'll bite." He looked at Grace and asked, *"Misleading?* Really, how so?"

"Well," Grace began, "if Darwin's theory was based solely on natural selection, I'd be fine with it, but . . ." Grace's voice trailed off as she looked around the room. *Not here*, she thought. *They don't want to hear this here.*

But Mr. Livingston was intrigued now. "But what?"

Grace hesitated, hoping to find a way to wrap the discussion up quickly. "I think we all agree that there is variability *within* species based on environmental conditions. But—personally—I think Darwin used his theory incorrectly to explain the origin of species. You can't take changes within a species and generalize them to prove one species will eventual turn into another using the same process. Nor can it—no offense again, Cisco—so easily be used as an explanation for change in other fields of study, especially social sciences where there are always more variables you can't control."

A look of bewilderment spread slowly across Mr. Livingston's face. "That's fascinating. Do you care to elaborate?"

"Now?" Grace dodged.

Mr. Livingston looked at his watch. "We've got time."

"In front of the class?"

"Sure. We'll have you and Cisco debate each other." Mr. Livingston said this as though it were a great idea. He winked at Cisco.

Cisco picked up the gauntlet immediately. "I'm in." Jesse sat in the desk just in front of Cisco and held a hand up to him. Cisco high-fived him.

"I'm . . . not so sure . . ." The class responded by clucking like chickens. Grace smiled with a little laugh. "Okay, okay."

As the class cheered, Mr. Livingston bent down to confide in Cisco before he went to the front of the room. "Cisco, your paper on Darwinism was brilliant. Let her have it." He gave him a pat on the back as he headed to the front of the room.

Mr. Livingston announced to the class, "The proposition is: 'Evolution explains the origin of life.' Mr. Diaz will be arguing the affirmative. Ms. Davis, in the negative."

* * * * *

Bobbi approached the desk in the medical clinic tentatively. She looked over the half-empty waiting room, fearful she might see someone she knew. She didn't recognize anyone. She stepped up to the receptionist and announced, "I'd like to see a doctor."

The receptionist looked up from her computer screen. "Do you have an appointment, dear?"

"No."

"Okay." She looked at her screen again, checking the schedule. "It looks like we can squeeze you in soon. What's your name?"

"Bobbi. Bobbi Ryan."

"How do you spell that?"

"Bobbi: B-O-B-B-I; Ryan: R-Y-A-N."

"Have you been here before?"

"Yes."

"Do you have some identification?"

Bobbi pulled her wallet out of her backpack and fished out her driver's license. She handed it to the receptionist, who looked at it, then back at Bobbi, then set it down, and started typing into her computer. When she was done, she handed the license back to Bobbi. "I'll pull your file," she said, indicating the waiting room. "Just have a seat. We'll call you when a doctor is available."

Bobbi smiled weakly and went to find a chair. Her phone buzzed in her pocket. She pulled it out and read a text message from her mother: "Sweetie, the school called. Where are you?" She turned the phone off and put it back into the side pocket of her backpack.

* * * * *

Mrs. Ryan walked up to the door of her husband's office with a laundry basket in her hands. The door was open, but she didn't step in. Instead she stood on the other side of the threshold, tentatively looking in. Pastor Ryan didn't like to be disturbed in his study, but this was important. She cleared her throat and said, "Honey, I just got a call from the school about Bobbi."

Pastor Ryan was turned away from his desk and computer, staring blankly out the window. He didn't respond.

"James?" she asked gently.

Still no response.

"James?" a little louder.

He didn't move. "Hmm?"

"You've been doing this a lot lately."

"What?" he asked, finally turning to her. "I heard you. The school called. What did they want?"

Mrs. Ryan shook her head. "They wanted to know where Bobbi was. She missed her first class this morning."

Pastor Ryan heard the words but seemed to miss the meaning. "Did you try texting her?"

"Of course I did!"

Pastor Ryan looked up at his wife. "You don't need to get short with me." He sounded a little perplexed and condescending.

Mrs. Ryan fought impatience. "You're going to lecture me on *my* attitude?" Her husband just looked at her dully. "You've been so preoccupied with church, you don't even see what's going on around here."

"I've got Jim Shaw breathing down my neck," he said defensively. "The church is running a deficit, and he stares at me with those beady little eyes every Sunday morning. I can't stand it!"

Mrs. Ryan pleaded now. "James, you're losing her."

"Losing who?" He was off in thought again, staring at a spreadsheet on his computer screen.

She knew better than to try to talk to him when he was like this. "Never mind." She lowered her head and walked away.

* * * * *

Bobbi found a seat next to what looked like a three- or four-year-old little girl rocking her doll. She had sparkling blue eyes and bouncy blond curls. Bobbi looked up to see the little girl's mother watching Bobbi admire her daughter, and they both smiled in acknowledgment. The woman had a round, full belly and was obviously expecting another child soon. Bobbi looked at the woman's belly nervously. The woman patted it, nodded, and exchanged smiles with Bobbi again.

Bobbi scanned the side tables for an interesting magazine. Nothing. She looked back at the mother, whose head was now down, reading something that appeared to have "family" in the title. Bobbi turned to the little girl. "What's your name?"

She reached for her mother's lap.

"She's our shiest child," the mother apologized.

Bobbi looked at her, a little surprised. "You have more?"

She patted her belly again. "This will be number five."

The little girl peeked up from her mother's lap, and Bobbi made a funny face. She turned back to hide again, laughing. The mother chided her gently to talk to Bobbi, but the little girl wiggled a "no." She looked back up at Bobbi somewhat helplessly.

Bobbi shrugged. As the woman cuddled her child again, Bobbi had a thought. "Um," she started tentatively, "can I ask you a personal question?"

"Sure," the woman said, looking back up from her daughter.

"Are you excited?" She couldn't help but let her eyes fall back to the woman's swollen abdomen.

The mother smiled awkwardly, then looked at her belly as well. "Honestly? Yes and no." She patted it again. "This one was a surprise—kind of like our first one." Her eyes looked a little glossy. "We're struggling a little financially, and having another . . . well, it will make things a little tougher." Then she ran her fingers through her daughter's blond curls.

The little girl finally looked up again, then showed Bobbi her doll. Bobbi took it and began rocking it. The little girl smiled.

The mother continued, "But the trade-off is having another miracle like this one." She locked eyes with Bobbi this time, and Bobbi fought off tearing up.

"Bobbi Ryan?"

Bobbi turned to see a nurse addressing the waiting room. She instinctively wiped her eye and then raised her hand. "That's me."

"The doctor will see you now."

Bobbi gave the doll back to the little girl, grabbed her backpack, and followed the nurse. The little girl's eyes followed Bobbi as she left. When Bobbi sensed this and looked back, the girl was making the doll's little arm wave at her. Bobbi waved back, smiling weakly.

They walked through a door, into a hallway, and into the exam room.

"Have a seat," the nurse instructed. "So what can I tell the doctor you are here for?"

Bobbi looked at her shoes. "It's personal."

The nurse nodded. "Very well," she said, looking at Bobbi's belly and then back at her face apologetically. "The doctor will be with you shortly."

Bobbi gave her an uncomfortable grimace. "Thank you."

* * * * *

"Evolution is change over time," Cisco began. "It's irrefutable, unarguable, and—*the truth*."

The class laughed at his enthusiasm.

"Now stick this in your pipe and contemplate this mind-bender: A measly two hundred years ago, most scientists believed the world was about six thousand years old and had a theory of creation that was something between Adam and Eve and the Greek stories of the Titans.

"However, around this time, discoveries started to be made that caused scientists to question previous beliefs. Fossils were discovered, including dinosaurs, and lo and behold, they found similarities among groups of organisms that suggested they might have common ancestors—that evolution had occurred. No kidding!"

Students again laughed as if on cue.

"Now, it was in the middle of this perfect storm that a young dude by the name of Charles Darwin"—Cisco made a heroic pose, pointing at the picture of Darwin as it looked down on them from above the chalkboard—"went on a voyage to the Galapagos Islands."

Getting into the spirit of things, Jorge began whistling the theme from *Gilligan's Island*.

"Darwin discovered these little birds he named the 'Darwin Finches.' Though close together in proximity, they were divided by open water too distant to cross, and these birds, over thousands of years, *evolved* differently based on their environment and the food available on their individual islands. This affected the size and shape of their beaks—birds on different islands, though the same species, looked quite differently over thousands of years of adaptation to their environments. From this, Darwin eventually postulated that such incremental changes, if given millions and billions of years, could actual lead from simple life forms to more complex ones.

"Darwin's theory of evolution is b-e-a-*u-ti-ful*. Why? Because species change over time and space, all organisms share common traits with other organisms because they share common ancestors. Evolutionary change is gradual and slow, but over time, it is very significant. This led the smartest scientists who live today agreeing that Darwin's theories of evolution are irrefutable, unarguable, and—*the truth*. Evolution is all around us, and it's happening all the time."

Cisco pretended to shoot two pistols and blow the smoke off their barrels. Then he put them into imaginary holsters on each side.

Mr. Livingston beamed. "Grácia? Your rebuttal."

* * * * *

Bobbi sat playing with a loose thread from the knee of her tights, staring at the wall.

The door opened, and a woman with a clipboard in her hand stepped into the room. "Hello, Bobbi. My name's Dr. Taylor." Dr. Taylor sounded British or Australian, but whatever she was, her voice was comforting. The doctor closed the door behind her, pulled a stool out from a recess under the counter, and sat down. "So what can I do for you today, Bobbi?"

Bobbi looked at the thread in her fingers. "I . . . I think I'm pregnant."

The doctor consciously relaxed, trying to appear neutral and objective. She spoke as evenly as she could, keeping her voice warm and professional. "What makes you think you're pregnant?"

"I haven't had my period in two months."

Dr. Taylor marked something on her clipboard. "Have you been sexually active?"

"I did it once." Bobbi thought back to that Friday night after the football stadium. She was sure she and Jesse loved each other. At least, she'd been sure then.

"Can you tell me when the first day of your last period was?"

Bobbi came out of her reverie and thought about it. She shook her head. "I don't remember."

"Were you sexually active at that time?"

Bobbi's eyes fell again and she nodded.

Dr. Taylor made more scribbles, avoiding Bobbi's eyes for the moment. "And did you use contraception?"

Bobbi frowned. "No."

More scribbles. "Have you had any symptoms?"

"Symptoms?"

Dr. Taylor looked up. "Morning sickness, breast tenderness . . ."

"Uh, I've felt like throwing up."

Scribble, scribble. "How long have you felt that way?"

"About a month."

"Have you had a pregnancy test?"

"Yeah, I did a home test, but didn't trust it."

Dr. Taylor fought the urge to sigh. "Bobbi," she said evenly, "we can do the test right now and take it from there. Okay?"

Bobbi nodded. "Okay."

TEN
GRÁCIA VERSUS THE STATE OF JOHN C. LIVINGSTON

Grace stood at the podium and flashed her smile at the class, then at Cisco. "Cisco, your argument is compelling . . . and true—*partially*. Species do change over time and space. For example, Eskimos who live in the far north have shorter limbs in order to conserve heat, whereas Africans who live near the equator have longer limbs in order to release more heat. Species do adapt to their environments over time, but as you know, Darwin didn't write a book called *A Change within Species Over Time*. He wrote *On the Origin of Species*."

John Livingston leaned against a table at the back of the classroom, listening. He unconsciously shook his head.

"Building on what he saw in the different finches from the different islands, Darwin theorized that if it was possible for species to change and adapt, perhaps it was possible for all species to have a common origin—thus the supposition that all life may have started from a single bacteria cell. According to this idea, this single-celled organism 'adapted' into a multi-celled organism and so on and so forth. Eventually everything we see today in all its complexity came—according to *On the Origin of Species*—from that first single bacteria cell. The argument of 'survival of the fittest' asserts that as that cell adapted to its environment over time, the strongest and most resilient adaptations survived, and the others died off. As was made popular in the *Jurassic Park* movies, 'Life found a way.' That single-celled creature found a way again—and again—until it emerged from the primordial ooze, learned to swim, walked on land, flew, and eventually evolved into intelligent life."

Chase looked around the room. There was a lot of nodding. While Cisco had entertained with his antics, Grace was methodically building her case.

"The problem with this adaptation—or 'natural selection,' as it is called—is it's limited to the genetic material it begins with. In order to make a new species, you don't just adapt to your environment; you actually have to change the structure of the DNA. They have to *mutate*. Chromosomes—and their number—have to become completely different." Grace paused. "For Darwin's theory to be true, scientists believe there would have to be billions of small *positive* mutations in the original single-celled organism's DNA to go from that first strain of bacteria to, say"—she looked around the room—"Mozart.

"Once again, if this were true, we should be able to find evidence of such mutations, and for as many millions upon billions of mutations that took place, the fossil record should have plenty of them. These have been dubbed, 'the missing links,' and, like the Higgs boson, scientists believed that once they had theorized its existence, if they looked in the right place, they would be able to find it. But that's just not the case—the fossil records show very few of these mutations, if any. Darwin admitted in his book that no such links had been found to his knowledge, but he hoped that one day they would be—"

"And they were, Grácia!" Mr. Livingston blurted out suddenly. The entire class spun in their seats at the sound of his voice, startled at the interruption. "*Archaeopteryx*," he went on, "the missing link between reptiles and birds; *Australopithecus*, the missing link between ape ancestors and humans—"

"Mr. L!" Cisco cut in. "You interrupted Grace. I don't think she was done speaking!"

Mr. Livingston blanched slightly. He shook his head. "Sorry, Grácia—sorry. Please go on." He sat back. His fingers began quietly tapping on the underside of the table.

"No problem, Mr. Livingston." Grace continued. "Since *On the Origin of Species* became widely popular, there have been several times archeologists thought they have found that missing link. I'm sure you're familiar with the Piltdown Man. He was found in 1912. Scientists thought he was a missing link. As it turned out, they had mistakenly combined the skull of a modern human and the jawbone of an orangutan. Then there was Nebraska Man, based on a single tooth. Scientists thought that he was a missing link. Little did they know that that tooth belonged to an extinct pig."

The class broke into laughter.

Grace was gaining attention. She was a terrific debater with her easy smile and engaging storytelling. "As high-school students, we don't always get it right, but, hey…." She looked at Mr. Livingston. "Scientists don't either." Livingston could see in Grace's eyes that she meant business.

Grace smiled apologetically, broke eye contact with Mr. Livingston, and looked around the room. "I guess the larger point I wanted to make is that Darwin"—she stopped again to indicate the pictures Mr. Livingston had placed across the front of his classroom—"and all the scientists before and after him *still* don't know how we got here. That first single bacteria cell had to come into existence . . . but *how*?" Grace paused again. "No matter what the theories say, to this day we can't create life from nonliving matter."

Mr. Livingston had heard enough. He readied himself to bring this nonsense to a close.

* * * * *

Dr. Taylor stood outside the door to Bobbi's exam room with her hand on the doorknob, but she couldn't bring herself to turn it. She took deep breaths and tried to focus through the disorientation. These were always the toughest appointments. She tried to imagine what it would be like to have an unwanted pregnancy—let alone as a teenager. She and her husband, William, had wanted so badly—if they had only been able to—*No!* she told herself. *This is not about me. It's about this young woman.*

She turned the knob.

Bobbi sat on the exam table where Dr. Taylor had left her. Her heels were bouncing on the step. She looked at the ground. Her jaw was clenched. The instant the door opened, Bobbi's eyes met the doctor's pleadingly.

Breathe, Dr. Taylor told herself. She came in and sat back down on the stool. She spoke slowly and evenly. "Bobbi, I, ah . . . I have your results."

Bobbi didn't answer. Her eyes just pleaded all the more.

Dr. Taylor looked at the charts and pretended to read, not really focusing on anything in particular. "The pregnancy test—it's come back positive."

Bobbi's face looked as if it were going to break into pieces. A single tear ran down from her right eye, and she made no move to wipe it away. "My mom . . ." She spoke as if drowning. "My dad's going to freak." The blood began to drain out of her face. "My mom—she's going to be so disappointed." She took a big breath against a sob. "My dad's going to lose his job!"

Dr. Taylor found a box of tissues on the counter behind her and passed it to Bobbi. As she did, she put her hand on Bobbi's shoulder to settle her. She spoke like a doctor again. "Bobbi, you've got a decision to make," she said as warmly as she could. "Have you thought about your options?"

Bobbi took out a tissue and wiped her nose. "No, not really."

The doctor crouched to look up into Bobbi's face. "I want to discuss your options with you." She waited until Bobbi could look at her again. "All the choices are difficult, so you need to think carefully before you make your decision.

"Now, one option is you can carry the baby to full term—and keep it. You can also carry the baby to full term and give it up for adoption. Finally, you can terminate the pregnancy."

Are you excited? Bobbi heard herself asking again.

Honestly? Yes and no, the woman had answered. *But the trade-off is having another miracle like this one.*

She looked the doctor full in the face. "What should I do?"

Dr. Taylor smiled weakly and shook her head. "I can't tell you what to do, Bobbi." She pulled a square of paper from beneath Bobbi's chart, then found another sheet that had a list of contact numbers on it. She wrote the information she'd been looking for onto the piece of paper. "There's a clinic that can help you with this. I've written down their address and phone number. You can call them and make an appointment." She passed the piece of paper to Bobbi and looked into her eyes again. "I hope everything works out for you, Bobbi."

Bobbi took the piece of paper and looked at the doctor again. The tears rushed back.

"Give yourself a few moments," the doctor comforted. "You can stay as long as you need. When you're ready, you can go." She touched Bobbi's shoulder and nodded, then slowly turned and walked out of the room. It was a fight not to throw her arms around Bobbi and cry herself.

* * * * *

"Grácia, have you heard of Stanley Miller?" Mr. Livingston asked.

Grace nodded.

"In 1953 he produced amino acids by shooting electric sparks, simulating lightning, through original atmospheric gases. Miller proved that amino acids could be produced without a higher power."

Grace looked at the ground for a moment, then back at her teacher. "Your point is well taken," she said, "but he controlled the variables to get the results he wanted, and . . ." Her voice trailed off a bit.

"Continue," Mr. Livingston prompted.

"Well," Grace began, "Dr. Miller had to remove the amino acids after they were created because the spark that helped form them would also have torn them apart had he left them. He also purposely excluded oxygen as one of the gases because the amino acids would not form in the presence of oxygen, even though the earliest rock evidence we have shows traces of oxygen in them suggesting it was abundantly in supply when life would have been forming."

OB shook his head. He couldn't believe someone was actually standing up to Livingston. He looked around the room, and Luke, the star football player, wasn't only listening—for the first time in his life, he was taking notes!

"Not only that, but is anyone aware of how difficult it'd be to form a protein even if amino acids were present?"

"Yes," Mr. Livingston said, impatiently.

Grace cocked her head to one side, acknowledging his answer. Then she addressed the rest of the class: "Anyone *besides* Mr. Livingston?"

Students looked around, shaking their heads and shrugging.

Grace looked back at Mr. Livingston. "Can I explain it to them?"

He looked at his watch and raised both of his hands as if apologizing. "Sorry, Grácia, we're running out of time."

Cisco stood up from his stool at the front of the room. "Come on, Mr. L. Give her a break! Let her finish!"

Mr. Livingston looked sternly at Cisco and then softened. He looked at Grace. He closed his eyes and nodded for her to continue.

She turned toward Chase. "Chase, can I borrow a quarter?"

He reached into his pocket and tossed her a quarter. She gave him a big smile, then turned to Josie, who sat right in front of her.

"Josie," she asked, "if I flip this coin, what's the probability that I'll get heads?"

"Obviously, one in two." Her voice was pure ice.

Grace seemed not to have noticed. "Right." She nodded. "If I want two heads in a row, that's one possibility out of four.

The formula looks like this: one chance in two to the second possibilities, or one in four."

Grace wrote, "$2^2 = 4$" on the board. "If I want eight heads in a row, the formula for that would look like this: one in two to the eighth power, or one in 256." Grace wrote, "$2^8 = 256$." "Do you follow?"

A few kids nodded. "To get 100 heads in a row, it's more than 10 to the thirtieth power—meaning it's more than one with thirty zeros after it." Grace wrote, "1×10^{30}" on the board, then "1,000,000,000 . . . You get the idea." Grace stopped writing zeros after nine of them.

She looked at Mr. Livingston and then back to the class. "The law of probability states that anything larger than ten to the fiftieth power *is not possible*." She looked around the room again. "Now the chances of putting 150 amino acids together correctly to form a *single* protein is more than ten to the 164th.

"That's a number with 165 digits in it." She paused and looked around again. "Why? Because you need peptide bonds between every amino acid, and there's a one-in-two chance that each bond will be correct. If it's not, then it doesn't form properly.

"To have a proper protein, you need 150 amino acids lined up correctly. To make things even more improbable, they need to all be left-handed amino acids, as opposed to right-handed ones. If you have even one right-handed amino acid in the chain, it won't work."

Jorge's mind was spinning out of control. "Grace!" he blurted out. "How do you know all this shi—ah, *stuff*?"

The class laughed, but Mr. Livingston's eyes narrowed coldly.

A big grin spread across Grace's face. "My dad—he talks about it all the time."

"For real?" Jorge asked again.

"Yeah," she answered. "He's a microbiologist." Again OB was dumbfounded. Even Jorge was engaged and asking questions. *Unbelievable!* He couldn't wait to hear what Grace would say next.

Jorge had had the bright idea to video the rest of the class using his iPhone. He quietly got it out and pressed record.

Grace looked at Mr. Livingston, and then the class again. "Has anybody ever heard of Francis Crick?"

Amy's hand shot up, and Grace pointed at her. "He discovered the DNA helix," Amy responded.

"Yeah," Grace agreed.

Amy smiled broadly, then looked over at Josie, who was scowling. Amy's smile disappeared.

"He said that life on earth was so improbable that it was probably founded by some alien form from another planet," Grace continued.

The class laughed.

Mr. Livingston had heard enough. "Okay! This is exactly what you people do!"

The class turned as if they had forgotten he was there. Jorge turned his iPhone camera toward Mr. Livingston, who was oblivious of everyone in the room except himself and Grace.

"Just because something seems so improbable, you immediately assume that it had to come from some *higher power*," Mr. Livingston shot at Grace.

Grace coolly shook her head. "No disrespect, Mr. Livingston, but from where I'm standing, it seems like your position would take more faith than mine."

The class let out a sigh of astonishment. Grace had slowly brought most of them to her side, plus they were thoroughly enjoying watching the master debater squirm. Mr. Livingston's tone was not helping his cause.

"You know what? You're so predictable!" he snarled. "Now you're going to segue into intelligent design! Right? That some 'higher power' directed all of this to happen?"

Grace shrugged. "How do you think we got here?"

Mr. Livingston's eyes flashed. "Scientists are working on that very question as we speak."

Grace looked at the pictures above her on the wall. "These scientists?" she asked. He looked along the line of pictures. "Entertainers, philosophers, artists, athletes, thinkers? You know, the first day I came into your classroom, I was intrigued by the pictures that you have on your wall."

Everyone in the room looked up at the pictures.

"I mean, why? Why them? Why this specific group of famous people so prominently displayed, seemingly looking down on us from above?" Grace looked at Livingston and raised her eyebrows. "Why did you select these people, Mr. Livingston?"

"You know, Grácia, I thought you might have worked that out for yourself." He looked up at the pictures. "I mean, come on, these are some of the finest minds that have ever lived. They were instrumental in shaping the very fabric of today's society."

"That's true," Grace acknowledged, "but you also share something in common with them."

"Yeah, what's your point?" Mr. Livingston spit the words out.

She looked at the pictures again. "They're materialists," she said, then turned back to look at Mr. Livingston again. "Like you."

"What?!" He was too angry to say anything more, and he didn't want to say something he would later regret.

Grace pointed to the picture of Jay Gould. "Jay Gould here said that Darwin's theory was inherently anti-plan, anti-purpose, and anti-meaning—and that Darwin himself knew this. Therefore matter is the only reality, and our whole goal in life is to pass on our genes to the next generation." She looked Mr. Livingston in the eye again. "Don't you find that depressing? That we have no more purpose here on this earth—in this universe—than to survive and procreate? I mean, what do you believe, if anything?"

Mr. Livingston looked at Grace with a penetrating stare. "You know what, I'm not going to let you get away with it that easily—how about *you tell me*?"

Grace was still calm and unfazed. Chase wondered if she'd realized she'd walked into a lion's den, poked the lion, and then offered it her head. She looked at the pictures again, then at the flag, then back to Mr. Livingston. "I think that at one point you were so certain that God didn't exist, but now—"

Livingston cut her off. "You know what? That's enough! We've listened to your little *probability* theory long enough. It's time that we, ah—"

"Whoa!" Jorge shot out. "This is way too cool! This is way too cool! It fits right in with what that long-haired French dude was saying!" The class gave a few uncomfortable laughs. "Like, I might not agree with what you are saying—because it really, really sucks, but—Mr. L, like, you will defend to the death Grace's right to say it. Right?"

A few in the room jumped in with Jorge and echoed, "Right?"

"Right?" Jorge yelled at the class.

"Right!" more said. Several started clapping. OB and some others stood to their feet.

"Yeah!" Jorge shouted.

"Hey! Hey! Hey!" Mr. Livingston called out. "Settle down! Sit down! George! *Sit down!*" The class froze, somewhat stunned. "Now!" he shouted again. "Holy smokes. Sit down!"

Grace's eyes fell. She looked at Chase, who was looking at Mr. Livingston. Sensing her eyes on him, Chase turned and raised his eyebrows, acknowledging this was dangerous ground.

The class settled back into their seats. Many looked down at their desks, cowering away from Mr. Livingston's outburst. Every muscle in Mr. Livingston's body tensed as he looked at Grácia.

"Grácia, I'm going to let you finish what you started, but make it quick."

"Thank you, Mr. Livingston." She looked apprehensive, but she decided she would finish what she'd started. "Guys," she began again, "could it be possible that God created everything? That he did so with amazing artistry and creativity and purpose? That everything from the male peacock with its brilliant plume to attract females, to"—she paused to think— "our fingerprints, unique to seven billion individuals on the planet—or the endless universe? I mean, all of this points to design, and—forgive me if this sounds overly simplistic, but if there's a design, there has to be a designer, right?" Grace paused again and looked at Mr. Livingston.

The anger had melted from his face. He looked at the ground in the middle of the classroom, biting his lower lip. A bit ashamed by his outburst—and being called out by Jorge, of all students—he listened. He thought about what it meant to let every voice be heard and if it was really what he had practiced all his years as a teacher. These were principles he'd used to safeguard the dignity in every student, but in all his time teaching, he had never really been challenged—until now.

Something about the way Mr. Livingston looked—there was a sudden vulnerability— gave Grace courage to be vulnerable as well. "Mr. Livingston, it feels like every time I speak about creation in this way at school, I'm either shut down, laughed at, or both." Mr. Livingston looked back up at Grácia for the first time since his outburst, and their eyes locked. "What about open-minded dialogue? What about the pursuit of truth? Abraham Lincoln said that 'Those who deny freedom to others deserve it not for themselves; and, under a just God, cannot long retain it.' It seems like there's only one worldview promoted at this school—and it doesn't include the G Factor."

The class clapped and cheered as the bell rang. Mr. Livingston stood at the back of the room without saying a word as students filed out.

He didn't move again until long after the room was empty and students for his next class began filing in.

ELEVEN
FALLOUT

"How did you come up with all of those *facts*?" Chased asked.

"The look on Livingston's face was *priceless*!" OB chirped.

OB, Grace, and Chase were sitting at their usual spot in the cafeteria, eating lunch. The school had been buzzing about the debate most of the morning, and people had been treating Grace with a mixture of admiration and trepidation. Some thought she might get expelled, and others acted as if they wanted to pin a medal to her chest. Others just knew they never wanted to get in an argument with her. Some supported her desire to speak up for what she believed. Others were calling her a Jesus freak or worse.

"I mean, you were relentless," Chase said. "And how did you know all of that stuff about Livingston?"

Grace's usual smile was absent. She was tired of the subject. "I didn't," she said, shrugging. "I just . . . *guessed*."

"I wonder if your grades are going to suffer," OB said.

"You *guessed*?" Chase asked.

Grace slowly chewed her next bite. "Well," she said after swallowing, "the pictures on his wall went from atheist to agnostic, so I figured maybe his worldview might be evolving."

"I couldn't afford to talk to him like that. I am barely passing." OB punctuated each word by bouncing the hamburger in his hand.

"Talk about irony, though," Chase teased. "*Evolving* worldview? Eh? Eh?" He elbowed Grace playfully, and she laughed and covered her mouthful of food.

"It was epic," OB threw out. "Too bad nobody filmed it."

"Yo! OB!" Jorge came crashing into their table, almost sliding into Grace. She laughed. He pulled his phone out of his pocket. "No worries, man—I got the whole thing!"

OB and Jorge slapped hands, shook, and came away with snaps. "Dude, you didn't!"

"Yeah! Check it out!" Jorge held out the phone for them to watch. "I'm gonna upload it to YouTube right now! Livingston is *going d-o-w-w-w-n*!"

"Excellent!" OB agreed.

"Please don't," Grace pleaded.

"Say what?" Jorge exclaimed.

"Yeah," OB echoed. "Say what?"

Grace's eyes widened. "Guys, we can't make a mockery of Mr. Livingston."

"Why not?" Jorge asked.

"Yeah," OB echoed again. "Why not?"

"Because he's a good and decent man," Grace answered.

Jorge spun around on the table and sat down on the bench facing Grace. "Grace—and *closed-minded*," he said.

Grace shook her head. "He teaches from his convictions, Jorge. I don't have to agree with him, I just want to be able to say what I believe without being ridiculed. You know?"

Jorge pondered that. "Yeah, I guess you're right." His face twisted into a goofy grin. "Thanks, Grace." He popped up to leave, patting her on the arm.

"Um, Jorge?" Grace called after him.

He turned and came back. "Yeah?"

"It's not that I don't trust you," she said coyly, "but . . ." She held out her hand for his phone.

He laughed and tickled her palm.

She slapped his hand away. "Jorge!" Then she held her hand out again, cocking her head pleadingly to the side.

Jorge relinquished the phone.

"Thank you," she said. She took the phone, found the video, deleted it, made sure there was no backup, then gave it back to Jorge, smiling broadly.

Jorge nodded and walked away. Grace followed him with her eyes and then noticed Bobbi sitting alone, picking at her food absentmindedly. Jesse came over and sat across from her looking at his phone.

She turned back to OB and Chase. "Do you guys want to come over tomorrow night?"

OB's brow furrowed. "For what?"

Grace smiled. "A sur-*prise*."

"I hate surprises," OB said grumpily.

"I—love surprises!" Chase countered. "I'm in."

Grace turned back to OB. "OB?" Behind him, she noticed that Jesse and Bobbi appeared to be fighting.

Chase could tell OB was looking for an excuse. "Um, I can't! It's Cornhuskers night. They're playing Oklahoma."

Grace wasn't paying attention. She watched Bobbi as she got up, but Jesse was holding on to her arm. She said something and pulled away from him, heading for the cafeteria door. She was clearly upset.

Chase looked from OB to Grace and back. "Uh, OB, record it. Watch it later."

"Okay, fine."

Grace spoke as she watched Bobbi walk away. "Um, eight o'clock?" She patted Chase on the shoulder. "You know how to get there. Give him a ride?" She got up from the table without taking her tray and headed for the exit.

"Yeah." Chase nodded, but she didn't see it. She was already gone.

* * * * *

Josie looked up and shot daggers at Grace as she passed. "She's taken over the whole senior class," she said to Zabrina and Amy.

"It's like the rest of us don't exist!" Zabrina agreed. "And she humiliated Livingston—unbelievable!" she said incredulously.

Amy just looked at her food.

"Livingston was so livid," said Josie. "How dare she mock him in front of the whole class?"

Amy looked up, and both Josie and Zabrina were seething. Secretly she admired Grácia for standing up to Livingston and for sharing her convictions without apologizing for them. She wished she could be more like her.

Josie looked toward Grace again. "Yeah, she thinks she's so smart. Well I've got a surprise for her. We'll show her who's really in charge around here." She gave Amy a sinister grin.

Josie's words left Amy feeling empty, except for a slight sense of dread. Josie turned back to Zabrina to begin scheming together, as Amy's eyes followed Grace. She wondered how she had ever let herself get into the middle of these two.

* * * * *

"Who? What? Where's she going?" OB asked.

Chase just glared at him.

"What, Guv'nah?"

"Cornhuskers? Come on, man, you're an LSU fan!"

"Listen here, Chase," OB said. "Nobody wants to be a third wheel."

"Dude, you're not. Okay? You never will be."

OB munched on a fry, thinking. Then his face lit up. "Whoa!"

"What?"

OB motioned excitedly with his hands. "I just realized: Chase rhymes with Grace. Grace-Chase. That's freaky! This could be destiny."

Chase mimicked his enthusiasm. "Dude! OB—Kobe? Hey?"

OB immediately recognized the connection.

"You're gonna play in the NBA, bro!" Chase said. They slapped hands.

"Ya think?" OB asked, excited.

Chase shook his head and threw a napkin at OB, who caught it and shot it toward a trash can. Chase laughed when it fell short by a foot.

"What?" OB smirked. "Have you seen my moves lately?"

OB got up and pretended to bounce a basketball between his legs, then shot another napkin at the garbage can. This one was wide right.

Chase looked off after Grace and wondered why she'd been in such a hurry.

* * * * *

As Grace entered the hall, she looked both ways and didn't see Bobbi, but she thought she'd heard a door close. The women's restroom was just across the hall. She jogged over and went in.

Bobbi stood looking in the mirror. Her face was a mix of rage and strangled tears.

Grace slowly walked up behind her and waited for Bobbi to see her in the reflection.

When Bobbi noticed her, Grace smiled weakly. "Hi," she said. "I'm Grace." She gently touched Bobbi on the shoulder.

Bobbi looked at her in the mirror, and then caught a glimpse of a girl who'd followed Grace in. "I'm Bobbi," she said.

"I know." Grace smiled. "I've been meaning to find a chance to talk with you for a while. Would you be interested in getting a coffee after school with me? My treat."

Bobbi's eyes welled again, and then she took a gulp of air as if swallowing the tears "Yeah," she said. "I think I'd like that."

* * * * *

Principal Schaub sat in an armchair in the teachers' lounge across from Zach Brady on the couch. Alyce Hart, one of the English teachers, was grading papers at the table where Zach, John, and Bridgett Stevens usually sat during lunch. "You're doing a great job, Zach, a great job, and I really do appreciate it," he said. He looked at his watch. "But, ah, Barb has me on a very short leash, so I'd better get back out there." He got up to leave, offering Zach his hand.

"Thanks for your encouragement, Steve." Zach shook his hand. "I appreciate it."

John Livingston came in, yearning for coffee. He'd skipped lunch and buried himself in work in his room to avoid accidentally running into anyone from his debate class in the hallway. He wasn't really in a mood to talk, so when Principal Schaub passed him on his way out and greeted him, John didn't respond. Schaub looked after him for a moment, but thought better of trying again. The two men rarely saw eye to eye on matters, and Schaub presumed John had something on his mind. It was better not to push it at the moment.

John grabbed a to-go cup, put it under the coffee pump, and pushed. There was a low gurgle.

Zach apologized. "Oh, John, you're going to have to make some more. I think I got the last one."

"Ah, seriously?" John said under his breath. He set the cup down on the counter a little too hard, making Ms. Hart from across the room look up from her papers. John gave a smile that wrinkled no more than the corner of his mouth and held up his hand in apology. She went back to work without a second glance.

"You okay?" Zach asked. "You seem a little off your game."

John hadn't planned to stay, but seeing Zach there, he crossed over to the chair Principal Schaub had just vacated and collapsed into it. "I'm great, man—everything's great," he answered without conviction.

"Are you sure you're okay? You seem a little edgy." Zach sat forward from the couch and looked at John more closely. He knew that look. He could tell John was upset about something.

John shook his head. "Ah!" he admitted. "I got sucked into debating one of my students."

Zach tried to keep the amusement out of his voice. "It's debate class, right? Seems like the appropriate place for a debate." He sat back. "What happened to your policy about not sharing your personal feelings?"

"Yeah, I know, I know." He nodded. "I just got caught up in the moment."

Zach set his cup down on the end table beside him. "What'd you debate?"

John shook his head.

"What, come on!"

John shook his head again. "You're gonna love this." He sat forward a little, as if he wanted to whisper it. "Creation versus evolution."

Ears perked up at the table across the room, but neither of the men noticed.

"Really?!" Zach all but laughed. "What side were you on?" he prodded.

"Ha, ha!" John accentuated each syllable. "Funny guy."

"No, seriously, I can't believe you allowed that to be a debate topic." He raised his eyebrows. "You know, you'll probably have some parents calling."

"Yeah, you know, well, it wasn't my topic."

Brady looked at him, confused.

"You know, ah, the kids were debating the importance of marriage and Grácia Davis made an off-the-cuff comment about survival of the fittest. You know what? I didn't like her tone, so I convinced Cisco to debate her."

Zach looked even more confused. "I thought you said *you* debated her."

"It got a little complicated—I forgot to use my inner monologue and, ah, I blurted out a comment—she jumped on it—and we were off to the races."

Zach listened quietly.

"You know, I figured out what's wrong with her—" He caught himself. "I mean, what's different about her."

Zach shook his head questioningly. "And what's that?"

"I think she's one of you, mate."

Brady sat back and laughed.

Across the room a head spun around, but again, neither of them noticed. Ms. Hart caught herself and pretended to go back to work as quickly as she could. She ignored the paper in front of her and strained to listen.

"Seriously, though—seriously—come on." John held up a hand to change the flow of the conversation. "You know the pictures I've got on my wall?"

Zach wiped his eye as if the laugher had been too much. "Yeah, yeah—the famous dead guys?"

"Well, you know what they have in common, right?"

"They're dead?"

John shook his head disappointedly.

"They're famous?" he tried again.

"Ahh." More disappointment.

"I don't know." Zach shrugged.

John shook his head again. "Grácia knew. She pointed it out. They're atheists—they're agnostics. I hadn't really thought about that."

"So?"

"Come on, Zach! What would happen if you put up eight pictures of famous Christians?"

Zach looked at the floor for a beat, then back at John. "They'd probably ask me to take them down."

"Ya think?" It was John's turn to scoff.

Brady nodded awkwardly.

"You know, what got to me was she said that I was a—a—well, she didn't quite say it, but she strongly implied that I was *a materialist*. I was speechless. Have you ever seen me speechless?"

He shook his head. "No, no, not that I can recall."

"Then she had the audacity to accuse us—I mean, the school—of suppressing free speech. Can you imagine?"

"That sounds like quite the exchange." Zach leaned forward again. "She got under your skin, John. You gonna be okay?"

"Yeah, yeah." He appreciated the concern. Things suddenly felt more in perspective. "I'll be fine. I'll be fine."

Zach looked at the time. "Hey, I gotta get to class—but, you know, if you want to get a coffee after school and talk . . ." He nodded, letting the offer hang.

"Yeah," John considered. "I'll probably need something a little stronger than coffee, but that would be good, man, thank you."

"Okay."

Zach rose to his feet. "Well, take care, buddy." He started to leave, then reconsidered and turned back to John. He put his hand on his shoulder. "Oh, but first"—he paused—"I'm gonna go look at your dead guys right now."

John took a swipe at him around the chair but couldn't reach him. "Get out of here, you punk!"

Zach laughed and left. John sat back in his chair, smiling to himself and shaking his head.

TWELVE
ON THE ISLAND OF SOCRATES

Grace came downstairs into the kitchen, looking for a flashlight. She saw her mom painting with a glass of white wine beside her on the counter. Grace carried an old backpack she'd used in middle school that she now used to keep her journal, some notebooks she used for writing poems, lyrics, and thoughts, her Bible, and whatever she was reading at the time. She'd started calling it her "island backpack." She always took it with her when she went to sit by the fire pit or in the tree house on the island.

"Looks good, Mom."

Her mom turned and smiled. "Hey! Whatcha up to?"

"Uh, Chase and OB are going to come over to the island." She set the backpack on the counter and started sorting through it, making sure she had everything she wanted.

"Hmmm. Interesting," her mom commented. "Speaking of Chase—"

Grace stopped rummaging. "Yesssss?" she answered tentatively, raising her shoulders as she always did when her mom pressed her on personal matters. Her mom had that prying tone in her voice.

Her mom did her best to sound nonchalant. "Any new developments your mother should know about?"

Grace set her elbows on the counter and her head in her palm. Her eyes narrowed. "I love your subtlety."

Mrs. Davis didn't turn around. "You're not answering my question."

"Some people would call this meddling."

Finally she turned around, giving Grácia her "I know what you're thinking" look. "Has he asked you out?"

Grace dropped her hands to the counter and looked at them. "Mom, you know how I feel about dating."

Mrs. Davis nodded. "I do." She swirled around on her stool to face her daughter and reflected Grace's chin-in-hand pose. "Why won't you go out with him? I mean—no harm, no foul. He's *so* nice."

Grace looked up at her mom and her eyes narrowed further. "Are you listening to me?"

Her mom wasn't giving up that easily. "You know, when I was your age, I would have killed to have a guy like him interested in me." There was drama in her voice.

Grace laughed. "Okay, can you respect my personal choices when they differ from your own?"

Grace's mom reached across and touched her on the nose. "Why do *you* have to be so different from everyone else?"

"Hmmm." Grace looked up at the ceiling. "Because that's the way God made me . . ." She looked back at her mother, then reached across and touched her nose. "And the way you raised me."

Her mom laughed. "Okay." She reached over and pulled Grace's backpack toward her to get a better look. "Socrates? You sure they're ready for this?"

"Mom!" Grace snatched it back and stuck the journal deep into her backpack. "I gotta go prepare that fire pit."

Her mom let her off the hook. "Okay."

"Thanks for the chat," Grace said, gathering up her things and heading for the door.

"Love you, baby," her mom called softly after her.

* * * * *

OB stood at the door of Chase's house knocking. Mr. Morgan answered.

"Hey, Poppa Morgan!" OB greeted.

"Obadiah Zachariah," Mr. Morgan said in his singsong voice. He was one of only a few people who even knew OB's real name, and he loved to use it every time OB came over.

"Chase here?"

Mr. Morgan nodded and yelled up the stairs without turning around. "Chase!"

OB took a big sniff. "Your world-famous barbecue burgers?" he asked.

"Hot off the grill!" Mr. Morgan answered. "Come on in and have one!"

OB's eyes grew two sizes. "Thought you'd never ask!"

Chase came running to the door. "We gotta go, Dad, but thanks for offering."

OB put both of his hands on Chase's chest, stopping him. Then he looked at his watch. "Grace said eight o'clock. We've got half an hour to make a ten-minute drive—and I *need* one of those burgers." He pushed his way past Chase and into the house.

"Didn't you already eat dinner at your house?" Chase called after him.

"So?" OB answered.

Mr. Morgan put his arm around OB as they headed toward the backyard.

"Giddyup," OB squealed as Mr. Morgan let out his hearty laugh. Chase shook his head and followed them reluctantly. "We only have fifteen minutes, OB, so make it quick!"

* * * * *

Jesse listened as his call went to Bobbi's voicemail yet again. "Hi, this is Bobbi. Sorry, I'm busy living life right now. Leave a message and I'll try to get back to you in less exciting times. Wait for the beep!"

"Hi, Bobbi, it's Jesse—*again*. What, did your dad take your phone away or something? I wanted to ask if you wanted to do something tonight. Mom's working late at the firm and I'm here by myself. I guess I could go hang out at the indoor pool with all of those twentysomething babes, but I'd rather spend the evening with you." He turned up the charm on that as much as he could. "So, you wanna catch a movie or something at the mall? Your turn to pick." He waited a few seconds as if he expected his phone to buzz with her calling back, but there was nothing. "Okay then. Call me? I'll be waiting."

He dropped the phone on the bed beside him and fell back against his headboard. It was dark now. He hadn't bothered to turn on the lights when the sun had gone down. For a moment, he just sat there.

He reached over to one bedside table and grabbed the TV remote and his game controller, clicked on the TV, and started his PS3. While it was loading, he leaned over and pulled his laptop from the other side table, and found the tab to the walkthrough page he'd been following. Then he turned back to the TV, loaded his game, and picked up where he'd left off.

Jesse tried to ignore it, but he was angry. He mashed the buttons on his controller a little harder than he needed to and fought to care if he took out the latest monster or had to go back and restart the level.

Why's she acting like this? It's not like I did anything. He couldn't help but think back to that night in September—the last time things were really going well between them. Actually, things had been *really* good between them back then. What had gone wrong? They'd just done what people in love do, right? Wasn't that the way it was supposed to be? Wasn't that what girls really wanted? To be loved and held? Hadn't she just been talking about their relationship going somewhere?

A twinge deep within his gut accompanied the memory of that night. He hadn't really meant for it to go that far. He'd gotten caught up in the moment with her, and it had felt good, but he still wasn't sure why she'd suddenly decided to go along with him on it. She'd always resisted before, but she acted like she wanted it too that night. He thought they were taking the next step . . . but now he wasn't sure.

Countering slightly too late, the monstrous warrior his character was fighting landed a punishing blow. The screen darkened, and red letters on a black ribbon across the middle told him emphatically in all caps: YOU DIED.

He wanted to throw the controller across the room, but instead he dropped it beside his laptop and picked up his phone. No messages. He looked at the time: 7:38. He had no idea when his mom would be home, and he was getting hungry. He decided he'd go make himself something to eat. On the way he started dialing Bobbi's number one more time, just in case this time she picked up.

She didn't.

* * * * *

OB wiped the last of the barbecue sauce from his chin and then licked his fingers. Chase's family was gathered around the picnic table eating with OB—except Chase. OB looked back at Mr. Morgan and said nonchalantly, "I knew a woman who owned a Taser once—boy, was she stunning!"

They all laughed as one—except Chase again. He'd seen this movie before, and he didn't like it. Every time OB and his dad got together they'd wind up in a pun-off. Mr. Morgan thought they were "punny," but Chase never laughed. He didn't get how the two of them found each other so hysterical.

Mr. Morgan countered. "I was going to buy a book on phobias, but I was afraid it wouldn't help me."

More laughter. Chase looked at his watch. "OB, let's go."

Mr. Morgan held up his hand for Chase to hang on. "What do you call a pastor in Berlin?" he asked OB.

OB shrugged.

"A German shepherd!"

OB slapped the table laughing. "*A German shepherd!* Mr. M, we've got to do this more often."

Chase shook his head. "No, you don't. Come on. Grace is waiting!" He pulled his iPhone out to check the time again and got up.

OB rose slowly, but before he stepped away, he looked at Chase's dad again and asked, "Where in the Bible is baseball mentioned?"

Mr. Morgan shrugged. "I don't know."

"Genesis 1:1: '*In the big inning . . .*'"

Mr. Morgan laughed with his hands on his stomach like Santa Claus. He shot back, "Okay, then, what kind of car did the apostles drive?"

OB shrugged, too anxious for the next punch line to try to guess.

"A Honda. '*They were in one Accord . . .*'"

Chase grabbed OB by the shirt to pull him away. Olivia seemed near hysterics.

OB had to get in one more. "How do you make antifreeze?" He waited a beat. "Steal her coat!"

Olivia fell of the bench laughing, and the entire group laughed all the harder. Chase continued to lead OB toward the front of the house.

"Thanks for the burger!" OB called as they went through the gate. "Later, Mom and Pop Morgan! Olivia!"

The gate slapped shut behind them as OB gave the Morgans a regal bow and Chase continued pulling him toward the jeep.

* * * * *

The island behind the Davises' new house had become Grace's favorite place on the property, even as the weather grew colder. It was wooded, so she couldn't see any of the neighbors, and it made her feel as though she were deep in a forest away from everything. Sometimes she even pretended it was Terabithia from the stories.

There was a tree house and a huge pile of wood for the fire pit. Jonah had claimed the tree house, so Grace claimed the fire pit. They'd spent hours on Saturdays splitting the space between them, each able to be in their own worlds but together at the same time. Grace got used to hearing Hannah Banana laughing as she and her brother played games in the tree house. She'd strum on her guitar, scribbling down chords and lyrics in one of her notebooks as they came to her.

The evenings, however, when the fire pit was the nicest, had belonged to Grace alone. Chase and OB were the first guests she'd invited to share it.

Grace held Socrates in her hand, and OB and Chase sat in lawn chairs on either side of her, watching the fire. "When I was twelve," she said, "my parents got me this to write my thoughts and dreams in. I call it 'Socrates.'" She smiled at Chase, then at OB as well.

"The famous Greek philosopher Mr. B always talks about," Chase noted.

"Yep." Grace nodded. "I love his quote, 'Great minds discuss ideas, average minds discuss events, weak minds discuss—'"

"'People,'" Chase finished. "I like that one."

Grace nodded again.

OB sighed loudly. Neither of the other two seemed to notice.

"Read something for us," Chase asked.

OB wriggled uncomfortably, trying not to feel like the third wheel he knew he was.

Grace opened her journal and started fingering through the pages. "Let's see. Hmm," she said, stopping at an entry. "I wrote this when I was fourteen:

"Why was I born?
Why was I born a human and not an animal?
Why was I born in America and not a Third
World country?
Why was I born into a Christian family and not
a Hindu family?
Why was I born?"

OB suddenly had a thought. "Oh yeah—*existentialism*," he commented, lifting a finger in the air as if giving a lecture.

"Big word, OB," Grace said. "I'm impressed."

OB grabbed the edges of his hoodie, trying to look dignified. "Hey, ah, you know, my man Chase over here does spoken-word poetry."

"Get out of here!" Grace said, looking at Chase.

"Seriously," OB confirmed.

Grace looked at Chase with a hint of admiration. "Can you recite something for me?"

Chase stiffened.

"Come on, man," OB goaded. "Pretend we're not here."

Chase scratched his forehead. "All right." He stood up and circled to the other side of the fire pit. He took a deep breath to calm his nerves and began:

> "We look up to losers, we become users,
> beggars can't become choosers, we buy what
> they sell us,
> they tell us, live your life, make everybody
> jealous!
> See, we think that heaven's made of
> fine white powder, that fulfillment's found in a
> pair of dice,
> and that the path to paradise is paved with weed
> and dollar bills.
> It's the green brick road that we're on and we're
> the tin men and women.
> We've lost our heart to the illusion called
> prosperity,
> we encourage barbarity, while we slay the knight
> called chivalry
> and after a night that you can't even remember,
> you wake up
> to a girl you've never met, so you run.
> But fate must not be blessin' you, because you
> run into the guys
> you owe money to and with one shot,
> you leave behind a smoking barrel, a girl with a
> new life inside her,

and a wound no one can mend. Because the
baby
grows up wondering why he can't even call his
father a friend
and so the cycle starts again. But that's just the
way it is, right?
We all gotta live life. We all live and die.
No day is different than this night. We all die
under starlight,
an' it doesn't matter what you fight
an' that's just the way it is, right?
An' that's just the way it is, right?"

OB and Grace looked at each other, mouths wide open. "That—was—beautiful, Chase," Grace said. "Have you ever shared that at school?"

Chase shook his head and gave her a look as if she were crazy.

"What?" Grace asked. "Why not?"

"You said it—Livingston's class."

"What? They will ridicule you?"

Chase nodded, and OB pointed at Chase in agreement.

Grace reached over and took Chase's hand in hers and patted it. "You're wrong," she said. "This would win you respect." Then she left her hand sitting on top of his.

OB looked over at Grace's sudden show of affection and raised his eyebrows. Chase was just enjoying the moment as they went back to watching the fire.

THIRTEEN
THE MOST INFLUENTIAL PERSON IN HISTORY

"Okay, let's take a break from the Constitution for a minute," Mr. Brady told his class.

Students sighed. Someone in the back said, "Hallelujah!"

Mr. Brady smiled. "I was watching the Biography Channel last night—" He held his hands up as some started to make faces and snicker. "I know, I know, I'm boring.

"But it really got me thinking: Who is the most influential person ever?" He paused, giving people time to collect their thoughts. "I want you to think about that for a moment. Who is the most influential person of all time?"

OB raised his hand while he was texting on his iPhone with the other.

"Obe?" Mr. Brady called on him.

"Steve Jobs."

"Why?"

He held up his phone. "Apple products influence every inch of the globe." He kept typing.

"That's actually right, Obe," Mr. Brady agreed, "and your grades are going to be influenced if you don't put away your phone now!"

OB's eyes grew bigger, and he slipped his phone in his pocket. He mouthed, "I'm sorry," to Mr. Brady, who nodded and went on to the next person. "Ally?"

"Gutenberg."

"Explain."

"He invented the printing press—he made books accessible for everyone, and books have changed the world."

Chase's thoughts began to drift as he thought about how he would answer the question. He began making the outline of a cross in the margin of his notes.

"Okay," Mr. Brady said. "Zabrina?"

"Confucius."

"I can see that," Mr. Brady nodded. "Somebody else? Kaley?"

"Aristotle. Think of all the writers he inspired."

Mr B nodded. "Amy?"

"Gandhi."

"Okay. Yeah, Cisco?"

"Martin Luther King Jr." He stood to his feet and started preaching, "I have a dream—"

The class laughed. Someone yelled from the back, "Amen, brother!"

"Okay, somebody else."

Chase wrote "Jesus" across the center of the cross and "Messiah" down the length.

"Josie?"

"Buddha."

Mr. B nodded again.

Chase circled Jesus's name in the cross, put his pencil down, and closed his eyes.

Jorge raised his hand excitedly.

Mr. Brady smiled, but was waiting for a typical Jorge comment. "Yes, Jorge."

"Yeah, Kurt Cobain, dude!" He started playing an invisible guitar.

Everyone turned to give Jorge a confused look. In the mayhem, Chase took a deep breath and began raising his hand slowly, with his eyes closed.

Mr. Brady's brow furrowed. "Seriously, Jorge?"

"Yeah," Jorge said, "'cause he's God!"

The class laughed again. Jorge was confused by their response, as he was being serious.

Mr. Brady shook his head. "Okay, I'm not even going to go there with you, Jorge. Anyone else?" He saw Chase's hand up. "Chase?"

The entire class was dressed in choir robes as he rose to his feet. He wore the suit and tie of a 1950s

*evangelist. As he prepared to speak, the choir rose
and began to sway back and forth, singing an old
hymn:*

*"See that host all dressed in white,
God's a-gonna trouble the water.
The leader looks like the Israelite,
God's a-gonna trouble the water . . ."*

"Chase?"

The choir continued:

*"Jordan's water is chilly and cold,
God's gonna trouble the water.
It chills the body, but not the soul.
God's gonna trouble the water . . ."*

*Chase raised his hands to quiet the choir now and
begin his sermon.*

"Chase!" Mr. Brady called again, then high-fived his upraised hand.

Chase was suddenly back in the classroom—no robes, no singing, no message on his lips.

"Is there something you want to say?"

Chase looked around to see the class staring at him. He wanted to share his thoughts, but he was afraid of what they'd think, so he lied.

"Can I go to the bathroom?"

Again, laughter.

Mr. Brady couldn't keep the disappointment off his face as he asked, "Can you wait? We have five minutes left of class."

Chase nodded weakly.

Mr. B turned back to the rest of the class. "It's a fascinating discussion, right?"

Someone threw a wad of paper across the room. Mr. Brady gave him a look, then continued. "Well, there's something that all the people you named have in common: They all have followers."

Chase leaned over so Amy couldn't see him erasing the cross and Jesus's name.

"Now," Mr. Brady went on, "back to the Constitution . . ."

The class groaned.

* * * * *

After class, Chase had his things together and shot out of the classroom before Mr. B could catch him. He couldn't believe he'd bailed like that.

Undercover Man strikes again.

"At this moment, your whole life is laid out before you." The words of the speaker from camp the previous summer suddenly filled his thoughts as clearly as if he were still in the camp auditorium. *"No one can choose what to do with it but you."*

The words hung heavier than ever. Instantly the emotion of that night flooded back, like a fire burning deep within him.

*"God has chosen you to be a piece of the puzzle that
is his plan for the world. It's no accident you came
to this camp this summer. God is preparing you for
great things. He wants the fire you feel within you
to be a light in a dark world. He wants to take you
and set you on a hill for all to see . . ."*

That night at camp, those words had filled him with such hope for the future, such conviction. *But now?* Now he couldn't even say Jesus's name out loud in public.

*He must have been talking about someone else. Not
me. Not Undercover Man.*

Chase jumped slightly as he slammed his locker and realized he was still at school. He looked around nervously, but everyone was too absorbed in their own worlds to notice he'd zoned out again. He checked his backpack to see if he had the right stuff for calculus, then put his hand on the journal he'd taken to camp.

How did that get in here?

He opened it to a random section and read the first couple of lines again.

*"He didn't fight to settle the score,
He fought for the poor . . ."*

He pulled out a pen, resettled everything else back in his backpack, and with the journal open in front of him, he walked down the hallway and made little edits on his way to his last class of the day.

* * * * *

Bobbi and Grace sat under a tree outside after school that afternoon. It was unseasonably warm for November, making it a nice day to be outside. The campus was quiet, with the sports season having changed from fall to winter, and all the activities had moved indoors. Even though Thanksgiving break started in a few days, it felt more like an afternoon in early September than late fall.

"I met Jesse in tenth grade," Bobbi was telling Grace. "He sat beside me in math class. He was a terrible math student . . . I take that back, he's still a terrible math student." She let out a nervous laugh.

Grace smiled.

"We were balancing equations and Jesse didn't have a clue. He asked me about them in class and after I'd explained, he shook his head, looked into my eyes, and told me I was smart." She worked at the edge of her skirt with her fingers. "Those beautiful blue eyes, curly hair, perfect smile. He was so vulnerable and . . ." She cocked her head to the side and looked at Grace. "*Gorgeous*." She blushed. "Then he asked me if we could go get a coffee after school and maybe I could help him finish the homework . . ." She looked back up into Grace's eyes. "We've been together ever since. It's been almost two years."

Grace nodded. "How do you feel about him?"

Bobbi's fingers fumbled together. She looked at them, then up at Grace. "I love him."

Grace took her hands. "How does he feel about you?"

She gave a painful half smile. "He's a sweet guy." She paused to think, but all she could manage was, "He cares for me."

Grace rubbed her hands together and wrapped her arms around Bobbi's shoulders. The chill of evening was coming on. "Have you told him . . . that you're pregnant?"

"No," she said. "I'm afraid he'll . . ." She couldn't finish.

Grace nodded. "Have you told your parents?"

"No, no." Bobbi could hardly manage words. She shook her head. "My dad's never liked Jesse. He doesn't trust him."

Grace looked at the ground and then back to Bobbi. She couldn't quite look her in the eye as she asked, "So, do you thinking you're gonna . . . ?" She let the question hang, unfinished.

Bobbi sat back and folded her arms tightly about herself. "When I was little, I thought abortion was evil," she said. She pouted and her eyes clouded. "But now . . ." She tried to shake it off. "You probably think I'm a monster, but . . ."

"No," Grace said, brushing Bobbi's braid off of her shoulder and then rubbing her on the back. "No. No, not at all." She shook her head. "You're in a deep valley, Bobbi."

They sat quietly for a moment. Bobbi wiped her eyes against tears that hadn't managed to fall yet.

Grace spoke slowly and compassionately again. "Do you believe in God?"

Bobbi looked up at her again. "With my whole heart," she said softly.

"Do you believe he knew you before you were born?"

Bobbi nodded. "Yeah."

"Then we have to believe that he has a plan." She looked Bobbi straight in her eyes, now glistening.

Bobbi grimaced again. Then she reached out and took Grace in both arms and hugged her tightly. Grace returned the hug, and the tears finally gave way.

FOURTEEN
A STAND AND A FALL

Grace, OB, and Chase were back at the island that Saturday night. Grace had invited them both via text. She said there was something she really wanted to talk with them about, but she couldn't say it at school. The evening was definitely cooler than the previous week's weather had been, and the fire pit was roaring high for more than just show. The air was crisp and clear. When Chase and OB arrived, Mrs. Davis told them Gracie was already out on the island sitting by the fire. They found her gently strumming her guitar. Her island backpack sat leaning against her chair, unopened. It wasn't late, but stars were starting to twinkle in response to the setting sun.

Grace smiled and greeted them as they came across the bridge, but she didn't stop playing. Sensing her mood, they both fell silent, appreciating the warmth of the fire and the sounds of its crackling and Grace's strumming. Each was soon wrapped in their own thoughts.

After what seemed like an eternity, OB broke the silence. "I'm feeling a funky vibe here."

Grace turned to OB and apologized. "Sorry, that's probably me. My heart's just hurting for someone right now."

OB continued: "What up?"

Grace thought for a moment. "Do you mind if I play something for you?"

OB noticed that Chase was staring at the fire, oblivious to their conversation. He smiled at Grace. "Please."

Grace began singing a song she'd been working on all afternoon.

> "You're in a deep valley, baby,
> Carrying the weight of the world,
> So if you're ever feeling lonely,
> Know that your quiet cries are heard.

> "The road ahead, it won't be easy,
> But please don't throw this life away,
> Your love will make it better someday,
> Believe me, it will be okay,
> He promised it will be okay."

They all fell silent again, listening to the crickets and the fire. OB nodded toward Grace. "That was nice."

Grace smiled.

Then they both turned to Chase, who sat with his eyes closed, head bobbing slightly as if still listening to the music.

"What's up, Guv'nah?" OB asked. "You look . . ." He thought for a second, looking for the right word. "*Troubled*."

"I don't know," Chase answered. He took a stick and poked it around in the fire, adjusting the logs. "I had this dream."

"Yes?" Grace encouraged him to continue.

He looked at the fire. "I was walking through the school, singing 'Your Love Is Strong.' And as I walked by the classrooms and through the halls, students and teachers, they . . . they started following me." OB gave him a stunned look. "That's right, they were following me! Afterward we all ended up in the gym, and I was like . . ." He paused and chuckled at was he was about to say. "I was wiping *words* off of people."

"*Words*?" Grace asked.

"Yeah," Chase answered. "Words like *shame, depressed, loser, judgmental*—"

"Huh. That's weird," said OB.

Grace looked at OB, then back to Chase.

"Yeah," Chase agreed. "So weird." Chase picked up the stick and started poking the fire again. "Then, today, in history," he went on, "Mr. B asked us who was the most influential person in the world and . . . I knew the answer. I even, like, wrote it down—I just . . . couldn't say it. It was like I was paralyzed."

Grace looked quietly at Chase for a bit as he watched the fire without looking up. "Chase," she said, "you may not see this, but there's something inside of you that's so inspiring. God really wants to use you."

"Huh!" OB scoffed. "The *guv'nah*? Huh! That's a good one, Grace. You crack me up."

"That wasn't supposed to be funny."

"Listen," OB continued. "God doesn't use people like me and him. No offense, Guv'nah."

Chase shook his head.

"He uses people like you. You're so—*together*."

"OB, you don't have a clue about who I am."

"I know what I see," OB retorted. "You speak your mind, you're intelligent, you bring people together."

Grace looked at OB for a moment, then over at Chase. "Is that what you see, Chase?"

All Chase could do was shrug in agreement with OB.

"I'm not perfect," Grace said.

"Well, you hide it well, Grace," OB responded.

Grace looked down at the ground while the two boys looked into the fire.

"At my old school, I couldn't find *one* Christian friend." Grace looked at Chase, then back at OB. "So I ended up hanging out with this group of people, and they were great— but they loved to party."

OB gave her an awkward smile of understanding.

"I felt like I could justify being with them as long as I was witnessing to them—I was their designated driver, and . . ." She trailed off. "Before long, I was convinced that just drinking on weekends was okay."

"Did your parents find out?" OB asked.

Grace shook her head. "They noticed changes in me, but they thought I was just going through typical teenage stuff. I was grouchy and tired most of the time. I treated Jonah horribly. One night after a bender I accidentally pushed him down the stairs." She grimaced at the memory, then wiped away a tear.

"On weekends I'd arrange to sleep at a friend's place so my parents wouldn't see me hungover." Her eyes began to well up. "I got into a relationship with this guy, who . . ." She shook her head as if trying to rattle a memory loose from her head. "He didn't share my same faith. We were drinking one night. . ." Her voice broke. She took a breath and unsuccessfully tried to swallow a sob. "I gave in to things . . . I gave in . . ." Her face clouded and a tear ran down her cheek.

OB gazed out into the night, as if not looking at her gave her more privacy. Finally, he asked, "How did you . . . how did you *change?*"

Grace smiled feebly and wiped the tears out of her eyes. "I met this *amazing* Christian girl named Bree." The firelight danced on Grace's face. "She loved *me*, in spite of *me*." Grace looked over to Chase and gave him a smile that only the edges of her mouth seem to notice. "She was my angel."

Grace looked up into the night sky for a bit, then back into the fire. When she spoke again, her voice had lost its tremble. "I have experienced God's grace in a way that that I can't explain."

"Is that why you're reaching out to Bobbi?" Chase asked her.

Grace nodded without looking up at him. "God loves Bobbi—he loves me—no matter what we've done." She looked at Chase again, then back at the fire.

Again there was no noise, but the crackling of the fire and a few crickets somewhere nearby.

Grace's words sank into Chase in a weird way. *God loves Bobbi—God loves me—no matter what we've done.*

No matter what we've done.

Suddenly the poem he'd been working on since summer camp started taking on new meaning. The words welled up within him. As they did, they began to turn in his mind with new cadence and rhythm, like a heartbeat.

Before he realized it, he was speaking them out into the night:

> "He didn't fight to settle the score,
> he fought for the poor
> and went to the parts of the city that
> the rich wouldn't even dare think about.
> He cured leprosy
> when it was considered sin to touch a leper,
> he saved prostitutes when
> the 'religious men' were saying 'kill her.'
> He promoted love above all when his kinfolk
> were itching to attack
> and he continued to promote love

when one of his best friends stabbed him in the
back.
He continued to have hope when the people
he had come to save spit in his face
and he continued to forgive when
his blood dripped down to the cross's base.
But when I say *Jesus*, you just see the chain links
formed
around yourselves for protection but your fence
is weak
because so are the connections . . ."

* * * * *

"The overwhelming historical weight of Jesus's
existence is not what makes me have this insistence.
I believe Jesus is the greatest man to have ever
lived because when my heart was failing me,
Mother Teresa did not patch me up.
When my depression was choking me,
Gandhi was not the one to show me love.
When I was drowning in my own imperfections
it was Jesus that brought me out of that pit.
Because when I was at my lowest,
I knew what brokenness sounded like to the
hopeless.
It sounded like a piano with all of its strings
that were ripped right out of it,

still looking perfect on the outside to its admirers,
but knowing the sound of its music would never measure up
to the symphony of perfection.
But that's when the carpenter named Jesus came
into my life
and took this dead heart of nature and made it
so much more alive.

But see, we all form chain links around ourselves for protection
but the reason as to why there is no question
as to who the greatest man in the world is,
is because I see this connection.
It's this beautiful silver piano chord,
between me and my Lord,
and it's the most beautiful melody the world has
ever heard.
It's a melody that Jesus offers the entire world—
because when I hear *Jesus*, I hear:
rhythm, *healer*,
harmony, *betrayed*,
timpani, *murdered*,
melody, *alive*."

Chase stood before Mr. Brady's class the next Monday,
finally answering Mr. B's question. As he finished reciting the
spoken-word poem he'd finally finished up over the weekend,
the class broke into applause. Mr. Brady came up behind Chase

and patted him on the back. Chase's eyes were bright with a mix of elation and relief. He thanked Mr. B and sat back down in his desk beside Amy. Amy clapped wildly, oblivious to both Josie's and Zabrina's vicious looks.

Josie leaned over to Zabrina and whispered, "Freak! It's time to wipe the snobby looks off of these goody-two-shoes."

Zabrina nodded.

"I've got an idea," Josie said, looking coldly at Mr. Brady and then over at Amy.

* * * * *

The next day, the Tuesday before Thanksgiving break, Josie, Zabrina, and Amy waited outside Mr. Brady's room before lunch until his class had cleared out and he closed his door. Zabrina snuck to a window to make sure he was alone. He stood writing some things on the board for his next class before going to lunch. Then she snuck back to where Josie and Amy waited around the corner. Amy looked apprehensive as Josie again ran through what they wanted her to do.

"Are you ready?" Josie asked.

"Guess so," Amy answered timidly.

"She doesn't sound ready," Zabrina said, looking at Josie.

"Amy," Josie prodded her. "What's the matter? Are you afraid?" She laughed unpleasantly.

Amy defended herself. "No. It's not that. I just don't get why we're doing this to Mr. Brady."

Josie rolled her eyes. "I literally explained this to you a million times, Amy. Chase likes Brady, so if we get him, we hurt Chase. If we hurt Chase, we hurt Gray-*sha*. Go!" She gave her a shove.

Amy walked over to his door, then shot a tentative look back at Josie and Zabrina, who both motioned for her to go on. She stopped in front of the door and knocked.

"Come in!"

Amy walked in, pretending to be upset, and closed the door behind her. "Hey."

"Hey, Amy. What can I do for you?"

"Mr. B, I need to talk to someone. You're the only person I could think of who'd understand."

Mr. Brady looked puzzled. "Sit down," he said. "What's on your mind?"

Amy sat, playing with a ring on one of her fingers. "I have a friend who I think wants to hurt herself," she began. "She just found out her parents are getting a divorce, and they are making her choose which one to live with. I don't know what to tell her."

"Hmm." Mr. Brady considered what she was saying. "I mean, that's a really tough place to be. And, um—a lot of kids are dealing with divorce now and sometimes—you just being a sounding board for them, and being there—that's really all you can do."

Amy nervously played with the ends of her hair. "Mr. Brady," she said. "I know you're a Christian." She folded her hands in her lap. "Would you mind praying for me?" She looked down again. "Just that I would, like, I don't know . . . say the right things to her?"

Mr. Brady considered this for a moment, then smiled. "Yeah, I can do that for you, Amy."

She smiled back and folded her hands again.

Mr. Brady bowed his head and closed his eyes. Amy took a quick look behind her to see Josie and Zabrina in position with Josie's iPhone. They nodded, and she bowed her head with Mr. B. Josie began recording.

Amy didn't close her eyes though. A sick feeling grew in the pit of her stomach as she looked at Mr. B and then at her hands folded in her lap.

"Lord," Mr. Brady prayed, "thank you for Amy, that she's been a good friend to someone who's really hurting right now. Please give her the words to say and may she comfort her friend. Give her wisdom and patience. Please be with this family that's making tough decisions If at all possible, intervene and stop this couple from divorcing. In Jesus's name we pray, amen."

At "amen," Josie and Zabrina ducked under the windowsill. Amy looked up at Mr. Brady again and gave him an uncomfortable smile. "Thank you, Mr. B. You're such an inspiration. God bless you."

"You too."

She got up and left the room as quickly and calmly as she could.

Once she got around the corner, Josie and Zabrina each grabbed one of her arms excitedly.

"Look at this! Nice work," Josie congratulated her. "Once Schaub sees this, he's *done!*"

Amy gave her a smile with no heart in it, but neither Josie nor Zabrina noticed as they turned to run down the sidewalk, giggling maliciously as they replayed the video one more time.

* * * * *

The speed with which Josie's video was acted upon may have set a record for bureaucratic efficiency at Eastglenn High School. The e-mail was sent anonymously from a Gmail account set up on a school computer in the library directly to Principal Schaub. Before the end of school that day, Amy was called in and asked what was happening in the video. As she had been instructed by Josie, she told Principal Schaub that she didn't know about the video, but Mr. Brady had been talking with her about God and asked if he could pray for her before she left. She said he'd been really nice about it, even though it made her a little uncomfortable. He hadn't done anything wrong, had he?

The next morning—which was the Wednesday before Thanksgiving and only half a day of classes—Zach Brady was informed he needed to see Principal Schaub. Though his story differed greatly from Amy's, the fact that they had video evidence of him praying with a student on campus seemed to be all Schaub paid attention to. Whether she had asked him to pray for her or not seemed immaterial. What had he been thinking? Did he understand nothing about the separation of church and state as specified by the Constitution?

When Zach tried to point out that the Constitution said nothing about the separation of church and state, but there *was* an amendment about freedom of religious expression, Principal Schaub threw up his hands. Now it was a legal matter that others would have to decide. He advised Zach to get legal counsel, and said the school board would be convened in a special closed session over the break to decide what to do next.

By the time everyone was going home on Wednesday, as was the norm for Eastglenn, the school was abuzz with rumors about what Mr. Brady had done. Most said something about the video and him praying with Amy, but some even speculated that it was more likely some kind of sexual misconduct issue.

When the word on the grapevine finally reached Chase, he dropped by Mr. Brady's room. Mr. B, trying to put the best face on things, told Chase he wasn't allowed to say anything about the situation until Principal Schaub said he could, but that it was really just a misunderstanding that he was sure could be taken care of before the end of the next week. It didn't take long, though, for him to figure out that Chase was honestly concerned, so he told Chase not to worry about it—especially over the holiday weekend.

"I'll pray for you, though," Chase said.

"I'd certainly appreciate that," Zach told him.

FIFTEEN
THANKSGIVING

With the Davises being new in town and without family in the area, Chase's mom decided the only proper thing to do was to invite them to Thanksgiving dinner at their house. Besides, she'd been looking for an excuse to meet the family of the girl her son had been spending so much time with. Not surprisingly, the invitation was warmly received, for many of the same reasons.

OB came over in the morning to hang out with Chase and play some video games. Mr. Morgan had volunteered to barbecue the turkey as they had the last couple of years, so as he watched over it, the three of them went out and threw the football around in the backyard. Just before noon, OB went back home to help his mom and dad with the things they were bringing.

The Davises arrived promptly at 1:00, the time of the invite, each of them with an armload of food. Mrs. Davis had spent the entire morning and much of the day before in the kitchen.

She decided to go traditional Puerto Rican on all of the dishes to add some spice to the festivities. She'd made *surullitos con mayo ketchup* (gouda corn-flour fritters with mayonnaise and ketchup sauce) and *coquito* (a coconut and rum drink, similar to an eggnog) to share before they sat down to the table; a sausage, pigeon peas, beans, and rice dish Grace told Chase was called *arroz con gandules*, but he could never quite pronounce it; *mofongo* stuffing made from plantains and fresh seafood; and Grace and Jonah made *tembleque de coco*, a kind of cinnamon-coated coconut custard, for dessert.

Somewhat flustered but with big smiles on their faces, OB and his parents—Dave and Tracey—showed up around 1:20 with a sweet potato casserole with marshmallow topping, green beans, and two rather dark pumpkin pies with blackened edges. She had left it to her husband and OB to take them out as she went to get ready, but they'd gotten lost in the Lions game instead. Tracey apologized profusely for the pies, she'd barely been able to save them, and Mrs. Morgan said it wasn't a problem because she and Olivia had made three themselves and she was sure they would be fine if they just chipped off some of the crust. "I'm sure the boys won't even notice," she said, and they shared a tension-breaking laugh.

For her contribution, Mrs. Morgan made the usual: honey buttermilk biscuits, mashed potatoes with greens, cornbread dressing with raisins and sausage, asparagus spears with a creamy cheese sauce, a kale and collard salad, gravy, and her mother's cranberry sauce recipe.

Though the Cowboys game was now on, it was a nice day, so the men gathered around the grill outside and the women busied themselves in the kitchen and dining room. The rest of the day was lost in chatter, giving thanks around the table, eating far too much, and the craziest game of charades the world has ever seen. Despite a strong showing by the team of Mrs. Morgan, Mrs. Zachariah, Mr. Davis, Olivia, and Grace, the team of Mrs. Davis, Mr. Morgan, Mr. Zachariah, Chase, OB, and Jonah swept the final round and edged them out. Everyone went home tired, happy, and uncomfortably full.

* * * * *

Josie Fullerton sat by the pool sunning herself, hiding her eyes behind big round sunglasses and pretending to doze. Though the sun was hot, it was not the reason she was seething.

The Bahamas with her family for Thanksgiving—*again*. And once again, every minute of it had been planned out for them like she was still nine years old. She was supposed to be learning to windsurf with her spoiled, six-year-old brother, but Josie wasn't up for babysitting. Besides, none of the instructors were even remotely cute. *Dweebs teaching dweebs,* she'd thought. Once her parents were out of sight, she ditched the dweebs and headed for the pool. Her dad had gone scuba diving, and her mom, as usual, was shopping—probably picking out something nice for little bro, and something stupid for Josie.

That woman has no sense of taste, she thought to herself.

The trouble was, the pool was deserted. She wished they'd let her bring Zabrina like they had last year, but they'd blamed Zabrina for that little incident of them being brought home at 3:00 in the morning by the local police. The girls had been more than a little inebriated—so Josie had to go it alone this year. After all, it was a family vacation, right? As if she'd ever seen either of them sober in the evenings during these "family vacations." *Yeah, right,* she thought.

Even with Zabrina there, they had fought and fought. She remembered lying in her bed and trying to cover her ears against them screaming at each other after they'd sent her to bed. *"She's just like you! Lying, conniving, scheming, manipulative . . ."* Her father's voice echoed in her mind.

> *"Oh, as if you even care about her! We go on these trips for what? So you can make it up to the kids for never really being their father? Father, that's what they call it—not 'CEO of the family'!"*

Josie winced unconsciously, trying to let the memory pass as quickly as it had come. She settled herself under her sunglasses again, feeling powerfully invisible to the world. The warmth of the sun felt good.

But she was bored. Her parents had a way of always making her feel bored. She peeked out from under her glasses and saw a waiter walking by with drinks for a young couple sitting at a nearby table. *Probably on their honeymoon,* she thought. *Blech! Chumps.*

She flagged down the waiter on his way back toward the bar. "Martini, dirty," she told him. "Charge it to our room." She flashed him her key card. "Room 1036." Her parents would never notice. One more martini on the bill wouldn't make a difference to them.

He looked at her a little apprehensively.

"I'm over eighteen!" she barked at him. "Don't make me go get my husband!"

He took the directions sheepishly, turned, and left.

* * * * *

Bobbi smiled awkwardly and scooped a spoonful of peas onto the man's plate. He looked back at her with a grizzled smile. He had a scraggly beard and was missing a tooth. He pushed the plate toward her emphatically. "More, please?" he asked.

"Oh, sure," she answered, taking up another spoonful and ladling it onto his plate. "You really like peas, huh?" she tried to joke.

The man made a few indistinguishable sounds and pushed on to the next server in line.

Her dad's voice came from behind her unexpectedly. "Go easy on those, honey. We only have so much, and we want to make sure everyone gets at least a first helping."

Bobbi rolled her eyes without turning around. "Gotcha, Dad," she said, dumping another spoonful of peas onto the plate of a woman, probably in her thirties, whose gloves were missing their fingertips. She and Bobbi made eye contact for an instant, and Bobbi's smile was not returned. "They took my little girl," the woman said.

Bobbi's eyes widened, and words caught in her throat.

The woman moved on.

Bobbi looked into the pot of peas before her and touched her stomach instinctively.

A voice woke her from her reverie. "Peas, please?"

She plastered a fresh smile on her face and scooped out another portion.

* * * * *

Jesse stood at the window looking out from the top floor of the One America Place building. From his vantage he could see where the Mississippi wound through downtown Baton Rouge. To his right, the Capitol stood tall against the horizon.

He wore a crisp white shirt, a thin black tie, his best black pants, and his most uncomfortable shoes. His sleeves were buttoned at the wrists. Behind him the room was filled with a cheerful rumble of small talk amongst the round tables, topped with white tablecloths and cornucopia settings. He turned as he heard his mother's laugh and found her standing in a group of three men, one in a suit, the other two in shirts and ties like himself, their suit jackets probably on the back of chairs somewhere just as Jesse's was.

"So, did your parents make you dress up for corporate thanksgiving as well?"

He turned to meet a blond girl in a velvety blue dress that ended just above her knees. He guessed she was fifteen or sixteen, and a white sweater covered her folded arms. She stood beside him looking out the window as well. He had no idea how she got there without him noticing.

"My mom, actually," he said.

"Your mom works for the firm?"

"Yeah," he answered. "She actually planned this thing."

"Oh, sorry," she said, giving him an ironic smile. "And your dad . . ." Her voice trailed off, but he was sure it was a question.

"Lives in California."

"Oh."

"With his girlfriend," he added without further prompting.

"Oh," she said again. This time more emphatically. "I'm sorry."

"Why?" Jesse shot back.

She turned, a little stunned, and Jesse shot her a smile.

"It happens," he said. "It's no big deal."

She smiled back weakly, then looked out the window again.

Jesse looked her over. "And your parents made you dress up for this too? That doesn't seem to be such a bad thing."

"What do you mean?" she asked.

"I mean, it suits you. You look nice dressed up."

She turned back to him and raised her eyebrows slightly. "Why thank you. And it suits you as well, if I do say so myself."

His cheesy grin was back. "My name's Jesse," he said. "Where are you sitting?"

* * * * *

Amy's father called down the stairs from where he was watching the Dallas game. "Is something burning?"

Amy looked up from her phone and for the first time realized a timer was buzzing. "Got it, Dad!" she called down the hallway.

She popped up off the couch and turned the timer off. A burst of hot air hit her in the face as she opened the oven door. She grabbed some hot pads and lifted out the turkey, setting it down on top of the stove. The little red thermometer had popped, and the kitchen filled with the smell of roast turkey. It was then that she realized her mother wasn't in the room.

She stepped toward the dining room and popped her head through the door. "Mom?"

Her mother sat in a chair on the far side of the table, holding something in her lap. There were tears in her eyes.

"Mom, are you okay?"

Her mother looked up and gave her a weak smile, eyes brimming. She held up a paper turkey that Billy had painted in bold colors.

"Oh, Mama." Amy didn't know what else to say.

"He made this just last year," she said. "I forgot that I had put it in with the good china so that I could put it on the table this year. And then just a few days after Christmas . . ." Choking on the words, she dropped the paper turkey into her lap. She wiped her eyes with both hands and forced a smile. "Who would have known I'd miss someone who drove me crazy taking care of him?"

Amy faced a smile back, her eyes filling as well. "We all loved him, Mama. He was never anything but happy."

Amy's mother nodded thoughtfully. "Always, always, always happy." She took a deep breath, stood up, and walked to a cupboard, placing the paper turkey carefully within. "I'll put it in one of his scrapbooks later," she said. Then, "My! Look at the time! Folks will be here any minute. Oh, and the turkey! It should be done!"

"I got it out, Mama. It's on the stove."

They heard a cheer from upstairs, and both looked up.

"Well, he'll be no help," her mother said. "Looks like it's up to you and me to carve the turkey this year. You want first crack?"

"Sure, Mama."

Her mother opened another cupboard and took out a bone china platter. "Help me finish setting the table first?"

They both smiled weakly and set about double-checking the table settings.

* * * * *

"Young lady, sit up straight when you are at my table," Zabrina's grandmother chided. "You look so nice in your dress. It would be a shame to ruin it with bad posture."

Zabrina's little brother shot her a smirk from across the table, but she ignored him. "Yes, Mamere," she said, dropping her shoulders back and sitting up in her chair.

"Ah, leave her be, Mama," Zabrina's dad said from the far side of the table. "It's Thanksgiving. Let her sit comfortably."

"Showing proper manners is ever uncomfortable, dear," his mother responded politely. "Such a pretty young girl would do well to know how to be a proper lady." She looked at him sternly. "But it would also help if you didn't let her cut her hair like a boy and paint it yellow."

He shot Zabrina an apologetic look.

"But Mamere, this is the fashion now. You can see it in all of the magazines."

Mamere looked at her granddaughter with eyes of compassion. "And that's the good thing about fashion," she said. "It never stays the same for long." She shook her head and murmured under her breath, "If only the girl had a mother."

"Mama!" her son spoke in a harsh whisper.

Mamere looked up at her family surrounding the table and ignored her youngest son. "Papere," she spoke to the other end of the table. "Would you say the grace?"

She held her hands out to Zabrina on one side and one of Zabrina's cousins on the other. Everyone at the table took each other's hands and bowed their heads.

* * * * *

John Livingston spent the morning reading at home, and in the afternoon he went to a local pub to watch a little of the Dallas game and have a pint. Having played rugby in high school and college, he'd always thought American football was a poor excuse for a man's sport—but he loved the enthusiasm of American fans. When the game was over, he went to a diner he frequented to have their "traditional" Thanksgiving dinner: two slices of turkey breast and one of dark meat, potatoes and gravy, cranberry sauce, green beans, and a slice of sweet potato pie with whipped cream on top for dessert.

When he finished, he checked his phone for movie times and momentarily thought about calling Bridgett Stevens to see if she might be interested in going to see something. Instead he found another number and dialed.

"Hello?"

John smiled. "Hello, Mum. How's the weather in Christchurch?"

"Uh, uh!" She called into the other room. "Billy, Johnny's on the phone, get on the other line!"

* * * * *

Zach Brady carried the baby seat into their living room and set it down on the couch. His wife came in to collect his coat, and Zach lifted the sleeping toddler out of the seat and took her upstairs to her bed.

When he came back down, he took the baby monitor off of the coffee table, clicked it on, and followed the sound of his wife, Heather, into the kitchen. He found her setting tea bags into two cups. The kettle was already on and starting to steam. She gave him a weak grin that held a hint of disapproval covered by a smattering of support. He got the message.

"I wasn't much fun at your parents' house today, was I?" he said.

"I think you did the best you could—under the circumstances." There was more encouragement in this smile. "So what are you going to do?"

"I don't know. Fight it, I guess. The union president gave me the number for a lawyer, and his receptionist said he'd call me back tomorrow morning."

"Why?"

The question caught him by surprise. He looked at Heather to see if she was joking, but her face revealed nothing but sincerity. "What do you mean? I've got to fight it."

"Why?" she said again.

He looked back at her, confused. "Because that's why we have laws—so we can protect ourselves and our liberties. We have to stand up for freedom. What's this country going to come to if we don't?"

"Okay," his wife said, glancing downward. "But is that what you've been called to do?"

At that moment the teakettle whistled, and they both jumped at the sound. They looked at it, then back to each other, and laughed. "That always gets me," Heather said. She reached over, picked up the kettle, turned the burner off, and poured hot water into their mugs. She handed one of the cups to her husband, then took the other into the dining room, where she clicked on the light and sat down at the table. Zach followed.

"What do you mean, 'Is that what I'm called to do'?" he said when they were both settled.

"I mean just that," she answered. "This is a good fight, and probably needed, but is it *your* fight?"

"Of course it's my fight. I'm the one who has been accused of something I didn't do. What do you mean?"

"I mean, is this the fight you've been called to?"

"I still don't follow."

She looked at her cup as it warmed her hands. "I mean, why do you want to fight to be someplace you aren't even sure you are really called to be?"

Now Zach stared into his own mug. Heather reached over and took his hand, bringing him out of his thoughts. "Honey, you mentioned that new charter school to me a couple of months back, and I noticed you've been to their website a half-dozen times in the last month. I decided to look at it yesterday. It could be a great fit for you. Their history courses have a strong focus on primary sources, their classroom sizes are small, and you'd get to work with underprivileged youth. Remember how you loved working in that inner city school when you did your internship?"

Zach smiled as he thought of the experience.

"And," she continued, "they'd love to have you as a quarterback and track coach." She paused. "You can't pretend you wouldn't be happier there. Maybe this is exactly what you needed to convince you to apply. They're looking for an experienced history teacher for second semester right now."

Zach shook his head. "I don't know. I don't want to just roll over for these guys. I'd look like I'm guilty. I should stand up for what is right."

"So you think the country really needs another polarizing debate about freedom of religion?"

"What do you mean?"

His wife patted his hand. "You know how these things go. You don't think the papers will get hold of it, and then the big news services? Sure, you will be in the right, but will it be the right thing to do? One more brick of division between conservatives and liberals, Christians and the culture at large. You'll be putting yourself in the middle of a media circus. If that's what God is telling you to do, I'm behind you 110 percent. We'll go through the fire together. But why endure something like that if it's not what God is telling you to do?"

Zach wasn't convinced. "I don't know, honey. I think I need to pray about it."

She patted his hand again and smiled at him. "I wouldn't expect anything less."

He smiled back.

"But for now," she said, "we've still got a couple of hours of a holiday to celebrate, so what do you want to do? Play some Pente? Watch a movie? Maybe some Chinese checkers?"

Suddenly a low moan came over the baby monitor, followed by sputtering cries like an old car whose ignition had just been turned on. Alisha was waking up.

They looked at each other and said together, "Watch a movie." They both laughed.

"I'll go get her," his wife said, getting up. "You find a good movie." She headed for the stairs. "No war movies!" she called back. Then from the top of the stairs, "And not *The Quiet Man* again!"

Zach shook his head and laughed. She knew him too well. He picked up his tea and went into the front room to find them something to watch.

SIXTEEN
THE VALUES THAT DEFINE US

Chase and Jonah stood talking on the bridge to the island. It was late afternoon the day after Thanksgiving, and Chase and Grace had just gotten back from doing some Christmas shopping together. When they'd gotten back to the house, Grace asked Chase to distract Jonah so she could sneak his presents into the house without him seeing—so he and Jonah had gone out to the island for a bit. Unexpectedly, the conversation had turned serious on him.

"Never?" Chase asked, incredulous.

"I think that's what she said," Jonah confirmed.

"Grace is *never* gonna date," he said, his eyes wide, "because she's into—uh—what did you call it?"

Jonah looked at him as if he was thick as a brick. *"Courtship,"* he said, holding up both hands to emphasize how simple the idea was.

Chase wasn't finding anything about this conversation simple. "Which is?"

"Do I have to spell out everything for you?"

Chase shrugged.

"Okay, listen closely," Jonah said, taking on the air of a sophisticated teacher trying to explain something to a twelve-year-old. "'Cause I'm not going to repeat it."

Chase nodded. "Okay."

"Gracie doesn't believe in dating, because it's an artificial relationship based on physical attraction. She wants a—a soul mate. Courtship promotes friendship, which leads to real intimacy. In essence"—Jonah put his hand on Chase's shoulder—"she wants to marry her best friend."

Chase looked into the water. He'd never heard of anything like this before. "How old did you say you were again?" he asked.

"Does it really matter?"

Chase shrugged again. "So, are you, uh, gonna court Hannah?"

"Heck, no! I'm gonna date her!" Then he winked and nudged Chase's elbow, smiling conspiratorially. "Just playing with you, bro."

They shared a laugh.

Suddenly Jonah's face turned to stone as he looked past Chase. "Sister alert!" he said, taking an imaginary key to his lips to lock them shut.

Grace asked suspiciously, "*What* are you guys talking about?"

"Guy stuff," Jonah dodged.

"Mmm." Grace wasn't buying it. "Be careful with this one!" she told Chase. Giving her best mom impersonation, she said it again. "Be careful with this one!"

They all laughed and started walking back toward the house. Jonah snuggled in between them and winked at Chase.

"So, kids, what are we going to do now?"

"*You*," Grace told him, "are going to go to bed."

"Ah! Come on!"

* * * * *

Jesse sat on his bed playing on his PS3 again. When his phone rang. He looked at it and immediately dropped what he was doing. It was Bobbi. He scooped up his phone and sat up to answer it. "Bobbi?"

"Hi, Jess."

"Are you okay?"

"I guess so."

"Okay, then," Jesse asked, "why have you been avoiding me?"

"I've just been thinking."

"About what?"

A silence fell between each of Jesse's questions and Bobbi's responses. *She's holding back,* he thought. *Something's not right.*

"Things," Bobbi said finally.

Things have been different since the night we . . . "Are you . . . pregnant?"

Bobbi bit back tears. "Yeah."

Jesse grimaced. He jumped up off of his bed and began pacing back and forth. "Bobbi, what are you going to do?"

"I, uh, I went and saw a doctor and she—"

Jesse cut in. "Are you thinking you're gonna . . ."

"Uh-huh," Bobbi whispered, no longer able to hold back the tears.

Jesse breathed a sigh of relief. "Okay. That's good. It's probably for the best, right? Right?"

"What do you mean?" Bobbi asked sharply.

"Well, I mean, like, wouldn't a baby kinda screw up your life right now?"

"What about you?"

Jesse shook his head. "What about me?"

"Well, wouldn't a baby mess up your life right now too?"

"Yeah," Jesse said, half-confused. "Yeah—I don't know! I haven't really thought about it. You just told me . . . And you're the one who's pregnant!"

"That's right," Bobbi answered. There was a long silence. "I'm the one who's pregnant."

Jesse struggled. "I'm sorry. I don't . . . ." His voice faded, and he waited for her to say something.

Silence.

"Are you still there, Bobbi?" He looked at his phone to see if they were still connected. "Hello?"

More silence. Then quietly, "Jess, I think we need to move on."

"*What?!* Wait, what are you talking about? What? Move on, what does that mean?"

Bobbi was crying softly now, her voice breaking. "I love you."

"Are you breaking up with me?"

"Bye," she said, shaking now.

"Don't hang up, don't hang—" The line went dead. "Bobbi?!"

Silence again.

Jesse threw his phone across the room.

Bobbi curled into a ball on her bed, her body convulsing with sobs.

* * * * *

Grace and Chase sat on a bench facing the small lake that circled the island. It was getting late and a little chilly, but the lights on the bridge and trees were too serene to leave just yet.

Chase looked toward Grace. "So, uh, Jonah told me that you're never gonna date."

Grace chuckled a little. "You believed him?"

Chase shrugged.

Grace looked out at the lake, then back at Chase. "I'm committed to friendship first." She nodded her head to the side. "Dating later."

"Really?"

"That guy I was dating in California? His name was Michael."

Chase nodded.

"Our relationship was all about performance. I felt . . . pressured to say the right thing, wear the right thing, do the right thing. . . all without knowing if he ever really wanted me for who I was—instead of what I could give."

Chase nodded again. He breathed in deeply and put his arm on the back of the bench. He spoke as if a little short of air. "I really appreciate and respect you for who you are, Grácia." He swallowed and looked into her eyes. "And, eh, your friendship means the world to me."

Grace smiled broadly, and Chase looked down at the ground.

Slowly, carefully, Grace intertwined her fingers in his. Chase sighed and smiled. She pulled his arm off the back of the bench and lay her head down on his shoulder, and Chase nuzzled the top of her head with his chin.

Grace smiled even more broadly when something occurred to her. She looked up at Chase for a moment with mischief in her eyes. "There's a six-foot alligator in our lake," she said.

Chase's eyes widened, and he began searching the shoreline as nonchalantly as he could.

"I named him Hippocrates."

Chase looked at her, puzzled.

"And I swore him an oath," Grace spoke, affecting the lilt and cadence of a Shakespearean actor, "that he shall hurt no one."

After a long pause, Chase shook his head. "That's weird."

Grace looked up at him with a big grin, and they both started laughing.

* * * * *

Amy sat in the dressing room, looking at the clothes hanging on a hook. Her sister, Chelsea, had helped her pick them out to try on. Chelsea had been dressing her as long as Amy could remember. Soon after Chelsea had gotten her license, the two girls had started a tradition of shopping together on Black Friday to buy presents for the family, but also to cash in on at least one sale for themselves. Amy wrapped her arms around herself even though the dressing room was quite warm. Her thoughts were a thousand miles away, and she shivered slightly. She felt as if she had a huge rock in the pit of her stomach.

What have I done?

After the emotion of yesterday with her mom, missing Billy again, and all she had been through in the last few days, it was finally hitting her. Josie had convinced her to lie to Mr. Brady and then to Principal Schaub. "It's no big deal," Josie had told her. "Brady will get a slap on the wrist, and Chase and Gray-*sha* will get stung."

That seemed small consolation now. If it wasn't a big deal, why did she feel so awful? Why did she let Josie and Zabrina tell her what to do? Why did she go along with doing something she knew was so wrong? She didn't want to hurt Mr. Brady, and even though she didn't like that everyone thought Grácia and Chase where becoming an item, she had to admit deep down that she didn't really want to "sting" them either. Not really.

Why did I go along with this?

She sat clutching herself, unsure of what to do next.

She heard a knock at the door. "Amy? Are you okay in there?"

"I'm okay, Chelsea," Amy answered. "I just don't feel so well. Can we go home?"

"Sure." Her sister's voice was full of concern. "Just let me go pay for these two outfits, then we can go straight home. Are you dressed? Do you want me to come in?"

"No," she said quickly. "I'm okay. Just let me sit her for a minute and I'll be out."

"Okay . . . You don't feel like you're going to throw up or anything, do you?"

Now that her sister mentioned it, she did feel a little like that—only it wasn't that kind of stomachache. "I'll be okay in a minute. I just want to go home."

"Are you sure you don't just need to eat something? You haven't eaten anything all day."

"No. I'm not hungry."

"Okay," Chelsea said, done with her medical checklist for now. "So, in the end, you like the green one?" she asked. "You like it better than anything in there?"

"Yeah, I think so. I'll try it on when we get home again just to make sure."

"Meet me out front when you are ready. I'll go get in line."

"Be right out."

She heard her walk away.

Amy sat quietly for a moment, looking at the dresses on the opposite wall again. Tears began to fill her eyes, and she stifled a sob.

* * * * *

Later Grace walked Chase out to his car. They stood quietly facing each other for a moment. "I'm so grateful for you, Chase," she said, then she threw both arms around his neck, rising up onto her toes to hug him tightly.

He slowly wrapped his arms around her and gave a gentle squeeze.

"Goodnight," she said, smiling into his eyes. She spun and ran back into the house.

"Goodnight," Chase said. She couldn't see it, but he was beaming as he jumped into his jeep.

* * * * *

Pastor Ryan sat in his chair in the family room, absorbed in a rerun of *The Andy Griffith Show*. His wife sat knitting on the couch. Neither seemed to notice that Bobbi was staring at them rather than doing her homework at the dining room table.

She was waiting for a commercial break, and when it happened, she got up hesitantly and came into the room. "Hey, Mom? Dad? Can I talk to you?"

"Sure," her mom said. "Come sit down." She patted the couch next to her, then whispered to her husband, "Honey, turn that down."

Her dad muted the TV and looked at her as patiently as he could.

Bobbi searched for words, unable to look either one of them in the eye.

"Good grief!" her dad said at last. "Did that boy break up with you or what?"

Bobbi bit her lip. "No," she said matter-of-factly. "I broke up with him."

He looked at the ceiling. "Thank you, Lord!"

Bobbi's mom shot her husband a disapproving glance, but thought better of saying anything. She looked back at Bobbi to offer her full attention.

Bobbi looked at her father, irritated to the point of bluntness. "I'm pregnant."

Her father's face slowly melted into shock. It took a moment for the words to register. "You're what?!" He sat up in his chair.

Bobbi's mom moved closer to her and put her arm on Bobbi's shoulder.

"You're what?!" he said again, his voice rising in volume as he stood from his chair. "You're *pregnant*?" He put his hands on head and began to sway. He was breathing as if he might hyperventilate.

"James, calm down," his wife said firmly. She turned back to Bobbi. "Just let her speak," she said softly, her voice breaking.

Pastor Ryan continued to pace.

"I, ah, I went to the medi-clinic two weeks ago and they confirmed it."

Bobbi's father had now passed from bewilderment to anger. "I'll kill him! It's that kid, isn't it?!"

Bobbi's mom rubbed Bobbi's arm consolingly. "How are you feeling?"

Bobbi grimaced. All she could do was shake her head.

Her mother's face began to break into tears as well. She reached to take her daughter in both arms.

"This is great! This is great!" Pastor Ryan said, speeding up his pace. "I can make the announcement at our annual general meeting, right after I announce that we're running a deficit. Oh! By the way, my daughter's pregnant!"

Bobbi's face steeled. "Listen to you!" She spoke clearly, punctuating each word with spite. "Everything is always about *you*! I'm pregnant, and *you're* the one who needs consoling?"

She spoke softly. "I hate you." Then she screamed, "I hate you!" and ran out of the room.

Again, Pastor Ryan looked on in disbelief, the wind knocked out of him. He looked at his wife, but she could only look at him with shock as she ran out of the room to console Bobbi.

What have I become? he thought.

SEVENTEEN
JUDGMENT AND MERCY

The closed session of the school board took place the Friday afternoon after Thanksgiving, with Zach and his legal counsel present. They showed up on time but were made to wait outside for forty-five minutes while the board met in closed session. When they were finally allowed in, Josie's video was shown and the board asked only one question: "Were you or were you not praying with that student, in your room, with the door closed?" Despite his legal counsel telling him he shouldn't answer until in a more formal setting, Zach said he had nothing to hide and that he was praying with that student in his room because she had asked him to pray for her. He didn't remember the door being shut—he always kept it open when he was in his room—but maybe she had shut it behind her when she came in. He honestly couldn't remember.

The board members spoke with one another in low tones after he answered. Then the board chairwoman thanked Zach and his lawyer for their time, and said the board would return to closed session for further deliberations. He would be notified later of their decision. She asked Principal Schaub to walk them out of the building.

Steve Schaub was stoic as he escorted them through the halls. He told Zach, "I'm sorry this happened," as a way of saying goodbye. It was hard to tell if he meant being called to the hearings or that Zach had done what he did, but before Zach could figure it out, his principal closed the doors behind him, locked them, and headed back toward the board chambers.

As it went, Zach heard nothing until he received the following e-mail late Sunday night:

> From: Steven Schaub
> To: Brady, Zachary
> CC: undisclosed-recipients
> RE: Suspension with pay
>
> Dear Mr. Zachary Brady,
>
> The school board will be further deliberating your case in the upcoming weeks; however, until that time, it has been decided that you should have no contact with students at Eastglenn High School until such a time as the school board deems it fit for you to return to the classroom.
>
> This e-mail is to confirm that you are being suspended with pay starting immediately. Please have any personal items out of your classroom

before the start of class tomorrow, Monday, morning.

This action is being taken because of clear evidence of you using your influence as a faculty member of Eastglenn High School to proselytize as clearly forbidden by the district employee manual, policy no. 249(d).

Please do not discuss this matter with anyone other than district officials and your legal counsel. To do so will be seen as a further violation of district policy and will further jeopardize your position.

You will be receiving a letter at your home in the upcoming week by registered mail confirming the information contained in this e-mail. It will also contain information about your rights in this matter as well as the dates of upcoming hearings.

If you have any questions, please contact Margaret Deveraux in Human Resource Services during normal working hours.

Sincerely,

Steven Schaub
Principal
Eastglenn High School

* * * * *

Zach came in early Monday morning, about an hour and a half before the first bell would sound. He cleared out his desk and took his John Stark bobblehead, but left most of the rest of the posters and paraphernalia. He'd get someone to retrieve those at the end of the semester if he needed them. It would be too strange for his students to come in to bare walls and a greatly altered environment.

John Livingston showed up about five minutes before he was ready to leave.

"Zach, this can't be true. This is crazy! There's no way they could have decided on something like this so quickly! Where's the due process?"

"Wow! There really is no keeping secrets around here, is there?" Zach tried to lighten the mood.

"What?"

"You heard already? How'd you learn I was suspended?"

"What does it matter how I heard? They can't just suspend you on some setup like this. That girl lied to you. You acted out of good conscience to help a student. How is that reason for suspension?"

Zach shook his head. "They didn't ask about any of that, John. They didn't even address it. They had the video evidence, and I did pray with that girl on school grounds. I'm not going to deny it. They interpreted that as proselytizing. As far as they're concerned, none of the rest of it matters."

John was irate. "Zach, you know this isn't right! What about your classes? It's only two weeks until finals! You have rights, mate. They can't do this! You're one of the best teachers I know. They can't just kick you out based on hearsay evidence."

"John, I've been wrestling with it all weekend. Regardless of what actually happened, I did pray with a student on campus. I admitted to it because it is the truth. As far as proselytizing, it's my interpretation versus theirs. And the truth of the matter is, I'm not sure I'm comfortable teaching in a place where this can be such a big deal—where I have to keep part of myself hidden, regardless of what the law actually says."

John's face was getting red. "I can't believe how calm you're being. I'm getting ready to rip someone's head off! We can fight this thing together! Let me talk to your lawyer. I'll be a character witness or whatever you need. This school needs teachers like you. This isn't right!"

Zach shook his head. "I don't know, John. I've looked at my legal options and I don't have a peace about it. I've spent a lot of time praying and thinking about this during the last three days. Maybe it's for the best. Maybe it's just time for me to move on." He put the lid on the box of personal items he had collected, looked around the room for a moment, then tucked the box under his arm. He held his hand out for John to shake.

John looked at it for a moment, then up at the ceiling. He wasn't willing to let it end so easily.

"Come on," Zach urged him.

John took his hand and shook it firmly. The two men locked eyes for a moment. Zach broke a smile and then slapped John on the shoulder. "Get to class!" he said.

As Zach turned and walked out the door, John looked around the classroom and at the banner across the back of the wall. "Beware of myth becoming legend and legend becoming history!" He shook his head and sank into a seat for a moment with his thoughts.

* * * * *

As Zach came down the stairs and around the corner, he almost collided with Chase.

"Hey, Mr. Brady! Almost took you out—sorry!"

"No worries, Chase," Zach said stiffly. He'd hoped not to run into any of his students before he was off campus, especially one he was close to like Chase. So much for that.

Chase saw the box in Mr. Brady's hands and knew the first bell was about to ring. With all the rumors that had circulated that weekend, he had been on his way to see his teacher before heading to debate. "What's going on? You're going the wrong way."

"Um . . . I, uh," Zach started, not quite sure what to say. He set his box down on the stairs, stalling. He cleared his voice and decided to level with Chase. "I've been suspended," he said. His voice was shakier than he'd hoped. "And, um, I'm not allowed to be here anymore."

The goofy grin fell from Chase's face and he looked confused. "Just for, like, the praying thing? Or what?"

Zach grimaced slightly. "You know I can't discuss it with you, Chase."

"So what?" Chase said. "You're just going to leave without saying goodbye?"

Zach didn't like the way that sounded. "I mean, I wish it wasn't like this," he said, knowing how inadequate that explanation was. He looked at Chase a moment more, realizing this could well be the last time he ever got to speak with him. He looked Chase in the eye. "Chase, you need to know, I'm so proud of you. You've found your voice. Your confidence." He put his hand on Chase's shoulder to let it sink in for a moment.

The first bell sounded. Zach realized he was cutting it too close and needed to make a quick exit. He tried to lighten the mood. "Well, you better get to class. You know how Mr. Livingston feels about tardiness."

Chase didn't move. "Thanks, Mr. B."

"Yeah," he said, bending back down to pick up his box.

"Hey, is it, uh . . . is it cool if I call you sometime?"

Zach smiled. "Absolutely," he said. "Anytime."

Zach gave Chase a half hug, then started for his car. Chase stood numb for a moment, looking after his teacher, then turned to run up the stairs toward Mr. Livingston's classroom.

* * * * *

Pastor Ryan sat at the kitchen island staring at his half-eaten bowl of Cheerios. Bobbi had avoided him since her announcement, spending most of the weekend locked in her room. She'd told them to go away when they tried to get her to come to church with them. Even his wife's pleas had been met with an adamant insistence that she be left alone. They'd heard nothing of her all weekend except quiet sobs through the door.

"Honey?" His wife's voice pulled him from his thoughts. He looked into her face and recognized the concern. She was wringing her hands. "Bobbi's not answering her texts."

He rose and took her in his arms. "It's okay," he said as she started to sob. He took her face in his hands and looked into her eyes. "Look at me. It's okay. I'll find her." He kissed her on the cheek.

"Okay, okay," she said, trying to collect herself.

He grabbed his jacket. "Call me if you hear anything," he said, and he headed for their car.

Mrs. Ryan leaned back against the kitchen sink. Her body shook with sobs.

* * * * *

Bobbi got off the bus at the stop the driver had recommended. He said it was closest to the address on the sheet of paper the doctor had given her. The day was gray and growing colder.

She started walking. Her arms were folded around her tightly, her eyes moist and bloodshot. She looked at the homes she walked by: yards of brown grass and weeds, houses that hadn't seen a paintbrush in years, chain-link fences with "Beware of Dog" signs, but no signs of life anywhere. She was a long way from the streets and avenues where she usually walked to meet Jesse or go to school.

This was new territory. Territory she would have to walk alone.

This will be for the best, she thought. *It can be like nothing even happened. This way no one will have to know . . .*

* * * * *

"Lord, please, please, please, please . . ." her father prayed as he drove, trying to get direction on where he should look for his daughter. His eyes darted back and forth, hoping for a clue. "Where did she go? Help me find her, Lord—help me find her."

Nothing came to him. *What do I do now?* he prayed.

EIGHTEEN
A FINAL STAND

When Chase entered the room, everyone was milling around talking in groups since Mr. L was nowhere to be seen. That was unusual. Mr. L was always in class before anyone else arrived. Chase thought he'd heard "Mr. Brady" being whispered about somewhere, but the voice trailed off before he could locate it. He caught a look from Josie Fullerton, but she looked away as soon as he turned his eyes in her direction. Grace was in her seat with her cell phone in her hand, texting. OB was in his seat across the room.

The door swung open and Mr. Livingston entered. Everyone froze in place as he walked to the lectern quickly, his face stern. Something was simmering beneath the surface. They were ready for the call to take their seats and start the day, but it never came.

"Ladies and gentlemen," he said, as if finally resolving something in his mind, "I'll be right back. Permission to mingle."

He turned and left the way he'd entered, the door banging shut behind him.

The buzz Chase had heard when he came in returned, louder this time. He looked at OB, who just shrugged. Grace had barely looked up from her cell phone.

Chase sat down behind her and tapped her on the arm. "Hey, what's up with Livingston?" he whispered.

Grace looked up as if she didn't even see him. He could see she was upset. "I don't know," she said. "But pray for Bobbi." She looked back at her phone.

* * * * *

A young couple walked out of the clinic quietly talking as Bobbi walked up. They spoke in low voices, not looking at each other. The girl pulled away when the boy reached for her shoulder, her arms folded tightly around her body just as Bobbi's were. They walked past her in stone silence.

Bobbi walked up to the door, put her hand on the handle, and hesitated.

She looked to the sky, then took a deep breath. She pulled the door open.

* * * * *

Adrenaline surged as John walked through the empty halls of Eastglenn toward the main office. He entered with a bang of the door. Steve Schaub's receptionist, Barb, was at her desk on the phone.

"Good morning, Barb. Is Steve in?"

"Yes, he is, John, but he's on the phone with—John—John!"

John didn't even break stride as he walked past her and into Principal Schaub's office.

"You can't go in there!" Barb called after him. "John!" she called again, rising to her feet.

The door to Principal Schaub's office was open, so John didn't bother to knock. Steve talked in a low voice over the phone.

"Steve, we've gotta talk—now!"

Steve held up his hand without looking up and continued into the phone: "It wasn't in the budget last year, and it wasn't in the budget this year . . ."

John slammed the door shut behind him. "Steve!"

Steve Schaub finally looked up and met John eye to eye.

"Steve! Right now!"

"I'll have to call you back," he said into the phone. "This is not a good time." He hung up. "John." He tried to sound causal and authoritative, nodding toward the chair in front of his desk. "Take a seat."

John didn't budge toward the chair. "What's going on?" he asked accusingly.

"I assume you're referring to Zach?" Steve asked.

John rolled his eyes and tried to be patient.

"Zach crossed the line," Steve went on. "There's video evidence—"

"Come on, it was entrapment!" John asserted. "Amy Daniels is just a puppet for Josie Fullerton and Zabrina Du Bois! Those kids were upset with Grácia Davis and Chase Morgan and they took it out on Brady!"

Steve Schaub hadn't gotten to where he was in the district by bucking the call of his superiors or disagreeing with their decisions. He'd been told what he could and couldn't say on this matter, and there was no way after a long weekend of deliberating with the school board that he was going to allow anything but that decision to be voiced. "He was caught praying with a student—*on the campus*. He knows the rules, and so do you, John! Come on!"

Their voices were loud enough that everyone in the waiting room outside the office quieted and looked at the door.

"Come on, come on," John shot back at him. "This is wrong on so many levels. Brady is the best teacher I know. He'd never jeopardize that by trying to convert students! This is a setup! It's just like he said: She asked him to pray for her, and they were there at the window with a cell phone. What?! You think they just happened to be walking by and caught that whole thing on video? Come on, you can't be that stupid."

Steve Schaub bristled but didn't take the bait. He sat back, cool under fire. He prided himself on not letting what others said about him affect him. "My hands are tied, John. The matter's being decided by the school board. There's nothing we can do here."

John put his hands on Principal Schaub's desk and leaned toward him. "If you don't reinstate him right now—*I'm done!*"

Principal Schaub tried to laugh it off. "You're overreacting to this whole thing," he said. "His job is going to be suspended—*with pay*, I might add—and there's every likelihood he's going to get the job back."

"Yeah," John acknowledged without a hint of agreement, "and if he gets it back, there'll be a list as long as my arm of things he can't do and he can't say. What happened to his First Amendment rights?"

Steve Schaub spoke with all of the authority he could muster. "I understand that you are Zach's friend and that you are trying to protect him, but you are going overboar—"

"That is not what this is about!" John fired back.

"Really?"

"It's about the freedom to be who we are inside and outside of the classroom."

"We all have to compromise, inside and outside—"

"Is that right?"

"Yes, that's right!"

By this time, Jose del Rosario had his ear virtually pressed up to the door listening. Barb snapped her fingers for him to come away, but he just held his hand up for her to be quiet so he could hear.

"What compromises do I make?"

"Oh, come on, John! I compromise, you compromise, everybody out there compromises every day—you know it!"

John stared through Steve for a moment and decided he was done arguing. "Are you going to reinstate him or not?"

Principal Schaub threw his pencil on his desk and glared back at John. He reached over to the hand sanitizer on the corner of his desk, pumped it twice, and made a show of washing his hands of the situation. "No," he answered emphatically.

John stood over Schaub's desk again. "You know I don't believe in God," he said, emphasizing his points by jabbing his glasses toward the principal. "But it's the biggest part of who Brady is, and I respect him for it. It's the reason he's able to reach so many of the students."

John waited for a response, but none was coming.

"You know what?" he said, taking his keys out of his pocket. "I'm done." He flung them onto Schaub's desk, threw the door open, and stormed out.

Jose barely had time to get out of the way before John Livingston burst through the door. Everyone in the office tried to look suddenly busy with other things.

"John!" Schaub called after him. "John! John!"

John slammed out the main office door and back into the hallway. Jose had his phone at his side, texting where no one else could see it. It didn't matter, though. Everyone else in the room was looking at the door John Livingston had just slammed shut on his way out.

* * * * *

Bobbi sat in the waiting room, checking the texts on her phone. One from her mom asked, "Where are you, honey?" The last one from Grace read, "Praying for you, Bobbi, hang in there." Bobbi swiped between the messages, wondering if she should answer or not. She looked up to see several people in the waiting room staring at her.

A nurse came through the door from the examination rooms. "Bobbi Ryan?" she called.

Bobbi looked up.

"The doctors are ready for you," the nurse said.

Bobbi rose and followed, putting her phone back into her backpack.

* * * * *

The debate class had settled into a quiet hum of conversation as they waited for Mr. Livingston to come back. Cisco's pocket vibrated. He took his phone out and saw it was from Jose. He couldn't believe his eyes as he read it.

"Hey, hey, hey! Listen up—Livingston just quit!"

The class gasped almost as one, then fell into a rumble of disbelief. "No way, bro!"

"Say what?"

"Get out of here!"

"You're crazy!"

"I'm serious. I just got a text from Jose," Cisco asserted.

At that moment, Mr. Livingston walked into the room.

"You're right, Cisco," he confirmed, going up to the lectern and taking a breath. He looked over the class until his eyes fell on Grace.

Zabrina looked at Josie and Amy and mouthed, "What?"

"Grácia," he said, "you were right as well. It seems that some people at this school have more freedom than others. That's just not right."

He picked up a folio that was sitting on the lectern and walked out.

The class sat for an instant in stunned silence.

Then Josie broke into a broad grin and clapped her hands. "Wow!" she said into the stunned silence of the rest of the class. "Brady and Livingston gone on the same day?" She went into full queen-bee mode. "Nice work, Gray-*sha*." Then she started a slow clap of her hands.

Zabrina joined in with a mocking laugh.

"You—little—" Chase began.

"Chase!" Grace cut him off. She looked thoughtful for a moment. "She's right. If I would have kept quiet, probably none of this would've happened."

"You know," Josie drove in, "sometimes it's better keeping your big—mouth—shut."

Zabrina gloated.

"You're the one with the big mouth," Chase retorted.

"Excuse me?" Josie shot back. She wasn't used to getting talked back to, least of all from a mouse like Chase Morgan.

But the Chase she thought she knew was a different Chase—not the Chase who now looked her straight in the eyes. "You heard me," he countered. "All Grace did was tell the truth." He paused, then went on, "You're a scheming, conniving, jealous . . ."

Grace turned away and hung her head.

"I mean, you made Mr. Brady lose his job. Everyone knows you're the one who made that video!"

"It was submitted anonymously!" Josie shot back.

"Right," he said sarcastically. "Who else would use Amy as a pawn?"

Amy looked panic-stricken.

"Amy," Chase said, "we've been friends for a long time. You're so much better than that! You really are."

Josie's look of superiority evaporated. Her father's words echoed in her mind: *She's just like you! Lying, conniving, scheming, manipulative . . .*

Grace's phone buzzed. She read it, looked up, and said, "Chase, OB, we gotta go." She collected her things and started for the door.

Chase got up and followed, circling around the front of the room. He walked past Josie, who still looked as if he had slapped her in the face. As he walked past Amy she mouthed, "I'm sorry," and Chase grabbed her hand reassuringly in response. Then he rushed off, following Grace and OB out the door.

NINETEEN
FINDING GRACE

Grace and OB burst through the outside doors, headed for OB's car. Chase had to run to catch up. "So, uh, what's up?"

"It's Bobbi, she's . . ." Grace stopped for a moment to weigh her words, but time was too short to be cryptic. "She's at the abortion clinic on Fourth Street. Her mom's been texting me asking about her. We need to go get her." She spoke, typing letters into her phone letting Bobbi's mom know what she'd just learned.

* * * * *

Pastor Ryan was still driving aimlessly, looking for Bobbi, when his phone rang. It was his wife.

He picked it up. "Hello?" He listened, took a deep breath. "What's the address?"

He paused for a minute and looked at a street sign.

"It's not too late," he said into the phone. "I'm close to there. I can be there in five minutes."

He nodded and hung up the phone. He was breathing heavily again, but this time not with anger. "No, God," he said with resolve. "Not this time." He stepped on the gas and sped down the street.

* * * *

A few minutes later he pulled up in front of the clinic and parked along the sidewalk. He jumped out and saw Bobbi sitting on the front step. When she saw him, she looked away. Then she stood to her feet. She began walking toward him slowly, ready for another fight.

They stopped about six feet from each other and he looked into her eyes. Her face seemed pale and expressionless.

"Are you okay?" he asked, his voice nearly breaking.

She wanted to be angry with him. She wanted him to yell so she could yell back—but this wasn't what she had expected. She felt a flood of emotions at once: remorse, anger, contempt, confusion, shame. She didn't know what to say. She stared at him coldly with her jaw clenched, then dropped her eyes to the sidewalk.

He shook his head. "I've got so much to apologize for, I don't even know where to begin." This wasn't the twelve-year-old who used to jabber at the table. This was his grown-up daughter. *How did I lose all of these years?* he thought to himself. His gaze was intense, concerned, and filled with regret.

Bobbi looked around at the ground. She couldn't meet his eyes.

"I wasn't there," he started again. "I ignored you. I got caught up in all my . . . my own selfish pride."

Bobbi locked eyes with him, her eyes silver and empty.

"I love you so much," her dad went on. "You mean more to me than anything. You're my little girl." He fell silent again, not sure what else he could say.

Bobbi grew fidgety again, and his head turned as if trying to catch her gaze. "I know I don't deserve it, but would you forgive me? Bobbi, please," he said again, searching for an answer from his daughter. "Please forgive me."

Bobbi's face dissolved into tears. "Daddy . . ." When she reached out, he took her in his arms. "Daddy, I love you. I'm sorry."

They stood for a moment holding each other. It was hard to tell who was crying harder.

* * * * *

When Chase, OB, and Grace pulled up, Bobbi and her father were still embracing. Grace got out of the car quickly, then slowed to a halt when she saw Bobbi and her dad holding each other. All three hung back, not wanting to intrude.

Finally the two separated, and Bobbi's dad cradled her head in his hand and looked into her eyes. He wiped his cheek, and then asked with a broken laugh, "When did you get so tall?"

Bobbi let out a small laugh that was still mostly a sob. She smiled at her dad for an instant, and he smiled back.

Once Bobbi saw her friend, Grace ran to her and threw her arms around her. Bobbi burst into tears anew. They held each other for a long beat. "I couldn't," Bobbi wept. "I just couldn't." She broke into sobs and Grace hugged her tightly.

Behind her, OB stood by the driver's side of the car, unsure of what to do. Chase walked over slowly with his hands in his pockets, standing behind Grace, but came no closer. He looked at Pastor Ryan, whose face was a mess with tears. He nodded to him, and Pastor Ryan gave a feeble smile and nodded back.

Grace felt Bobbi's body shaking and her tears running down onto Grace's shoulder. She wasn't about to let her go. Grace looked up to heaven and mouthed a silent prayer. She said, simply, "Thank you."

* * * * *

By lunchtime Josie was back to her gossipy self, and she and Zabrina were thick as thieves celebrating a successful robbery. They were in denial that anything they had done might have caused any harm, and they were already trying to figure out a way to get Chase and Gray-*sha* in trouble for skipping out of school in the middle of first period.

They hardly even noticed when Amy got up from the table and left, claiming she had a stomachache and was going to the nurse. The claim was only half a lie.

Amy walked through the hallway, dead to the world. She couldn't cry anymore. She couldn't feel anything. Numb and so, so alone. *I have a friend who I think wants to hurt herself.* The words she had used to entrap Mr. Brady floated back to her like a nightmare. She just walked forward, headed toward the front doors, toward the busy street that ran just beyond the front entrance . . .

"Amy?" The voice came from behind her. "Amy, are you okay?" It was Ms. Stevens.

Amy looked at her, broken and distraught. She just shook her head no.

"Sweetheart." Ms. Stevens put an arm around her shoulder and began guiding her. "Come with me. Let's go talk in my office."

Amy nodded and let her guide her down the hallway.

* * * * *

During the next two weeks, Eastglenn High School seemed to limp into winter break with its tail between its legs. Amy ended up confiding everything in Ms. Stevens, but embarrassed that it would get out that the school had acted to suspend one of its best teachers, the school board decided to offer Zach Brady his job back and put Josie Fullerton and Zabrina Du Bois on a probation that only they and their parents were informed about. One minor violation would get them suspended and jeopardize their graduation from Eastglenn. They were also instructed to stay away from Amy Daniels outside of class.

For his part, Zach Brady responded to the offer to return with his resignation. In the ten days the school district

244 | Because of Grácia

continued to deliberate, even despite Amy's confession, he had contacted the charter school he'd been thinking about applying to and they offered him the history position. He would start first thing in January.

John Livingston didn't miss a beat either, taking up a position at a local junior college teaching speech and debate. Rather than meeting in the staff room each day as they used to, John and Zach got together after work when they could to keep in touch. They also had a standing agreement that they would attend any event where Bridgett Stevens was singing. Despite this, John had still never worked up the nerve to actually ask her out.

At the end of the year, Bridgett Stevens also resigned from Eastglenn and returned to Baltimore to take a position closer to her family. Both Zach and John got invitations to her wedding a little over a year and a half later.

Regardless, debate and constitutional history were never the same. Luckily both were only semester classes and only continued a few weeks after that fateful day. Subs were appointed, but without lesson plans or really much of an idea what was covered over the semester, the classes were more social than business as usual, and neither had finals.

Bobbi and her family worked out a deal with Principal Schaub and her teachers where she could finish the rest of the credits she needed to graduate from home. Her relationship with her father improved in the coming months, but it was a slow healing process. He faced a lot of criticism at the church after he made the announcement to the board of directors that his daughter was pregnant. He agreed to a six-month unpaid leave of absence as the board decided if they would allow him to return or the church should find a new pastor. To help out, Chase's dad offered Mr. Ryan a position at the hardware store for the duration. Mr. Ryan took over the responsibilities Chase had fulfilled so that Chase could concentrate on college applications and finishing high school.

In the interim, however, the church board fell to squabbling over everything from the budget to who would preach each Sunday. Finally, sometime around the end of February, Jim Shaw and a group of others left the church to start another congregation across town. About a third of the congregation left with them. The remaining board members, unsure of what to do, asked Jim Ryan to come back and speak the next Sunday. He agreed. With Bobbi sitting in the front row, belly now bulging, he preached a message on grace and forgiveness that ended with most of the church coming forward to pray for renewal and to rededicate their lives. He was invited to speak again the next week and was eventually reinstated by the church board on April 1. The church began to grow steadily in the months to come. Pastor Ryan always joked afterward that having April Fool's Day as his reinstatement date was a reminder to never again let his work as a pastor get in the way of his relationship with God or his family.

Since Bobbi wasn't in school anymore, about the only social thing she did was start joining Grace, OB, and Chase on the island every Friday evening whenever weather permitted. OB usually volunteered to be the one to pick her up and drive her home. As the weather warmed, the group grew more and more excited about seeing Bobbi's baby. Early on, a lot of their discussions centered around whether Bobbi should give the baby up for adoption, and because she seriously considered this, she never wanted to know the sex of the child from any of the ultrasounds. After she and her parents decided she would keep the baby, she chose to keep the baby's gender a surprise anyway.

Over the course of that last semester, Chase tried to reach out to Jesse on a couple of occasions to keep him up to date about what was happening with Bobbi and the baby. Jesse seemed to appreciate it, but at the same time, he never tried to reach out to Bobbi himself. Bobbi was still very hurt about what had happened and found it difficult to even talk about Jesse.

Since Jesse was out of the picture, Grace agreed to be Bobbi's birthing coach. This took a lot of Grace's time, but Chase learned to roll with it, understanding it was a big part of who Grace was.

As things worked out, Bobbi went into labor about three weeks early—about a week and a half before graduation. The Ryans drove Bobbi to the hospital and Grace, OB, and Chase rushed to the hospital when Grace got the call. The three men sat in the waiting room and prayed for the health of the child while the three women worked together to see the baby born.

Bobbi was in labor for a little over seven hours, and she gave birth to a baby girl just before midnight. Though the child was small, she was healthy, and Bobbi was able to hold her for her first hours of life. She named her daughter Sarah Grace—Sarah after her grandmother, and Grace after, well, you know.

Bobbi was able to attend graduation with the others with relatively little sign that she had just been pregnant. Of course, her favorite picture of the day was her, still wearing her cap and gown, holding Sarah surrounded by Grace, OB, and Chase. The other was with her parents and her daughter.

Over the last few months of school, the four had grown rather close, and "Uncle OB" became somewhat of a fixture in the Ryan household—which, despite his new outlook, still took Pastor Ryan some getting used to. After graduation they still met at the island on most Friday nights over the summer— sometimes with little Sarah. It became a place for them to stay in touch, share their triumphs and struggles, and talk about the future.

Grace and Chase got into LSU the next year. Grace double-majored in political science and English as a precursor to law school, and Chase majored in history and speech. OB got a football scholarship at Louisiana Tech. It wasn't his first choice, which had been LSU as well, but he got to play football in

Louisiana, which was half his dream. He started at linebacker as a redshirt sophomore and was quickly dubbed by fans as the OB-literator. Bobbi opted to live at home and study to become a nurse at a local community college. When OB wasn't at practice or studying, usually with Chase and Grace, he was with Bobbi and little Sarah.

About two years after he resigned from Eastglenn, John Livingston finished the classes he needed for his administrative certificate. He found a position at the same charter school as Zach, replacing the principal who had hired him. Chase had thought about going there to do his student teaching before he graduated, but ended up back at Eastglenn in the same room that had been Mr. Brady's. Upon graduation, Principal Schaub offered him a position at Eastglenn and Chase took it. He would have to do something while Grace was in law school, after all.

* * * * *

Chase straightened OB's bow tie as they stood in one of the back rooms of the church.

"I don't think I can do this, Guv'nah," OB told him.

"You'll be fine, OB-Wan," Chase encouraged. He patted him on the arm.

"I've never done this before," OB confided.

Chase smiled and shrugged. "Neither have I."

"How can you be so—calm?"

Chase shrugged again, and smiled all the wider.

* * * * *

The buzz in the church quieted to a hush when the music for the processional started. Sarah, who had just turned four, was the flower girl. She came down the aisle first, then, once she'd gotten past the front rows of pews, she ran to her mother, who stood as the maid of honor. Across from her stood Chase and his best man, OB. Pastor Ryan stood between them.

The room was filled with old friends and family. Zach Brady was there with his wife and daughter, as was John Livingston. Olivia and Jonah were now teenagers. Jonah was no longer the runt of the family, but was now taller than his mother. Even Hannah Banana made it, though she wasn't hanging out with Jonah nearly as much as she used to. And no, they'd never dated.

When Grácia came into the room on the arm of her father, it was as if the rest of the room had emptied. All Chase saw was his bride. Her smile filled the room. For the next half hour, other than making sure he said "I do" at the right time and putting the ring on her finger when asked to, he could think of nothing else.

Then, at the end of the ceremony when Pastor Ryan announced them as Mr. and Mrs. Chase and Grácia Morgan, Grace and Chase shared their first kiss. It was a long, passionate kiss, and when it ended, Grace unexpectedly grabbed Chase's face and pulled him in for another one. She giggled, and he raised his arm and screamed, "Woo-hoo!" as family and friends cheered.

It was a fitting ending to a beautiful ceremony.

ACKNOWLEDGMENTS

I would like to acknowledge the investors who have supported the *Because of Grácia* film, this novel, and the curriculum, for their belief in this story and the power it has to impact this culture and inspire young people to live a life of faith.

ABOUT THE AUTHOR

Tom Simes has been working with young people for 35 years as a community leader, athletic coach, stage and film director, ministry leader, and high-school teacher. In 2005 he started a film company Five Stones Films. *Because of Grácia* is the fifth feature film Tom has written, produced, and directed. He is currently teaching filmmaking to eleventh-graders in Canada. Tom has been married to his high-school sweetheart, Michelle, for 33 years. They have four children, ages 16-26, and live in Saskatoon, Saskatchewan, in the heartland of Canada.

COMING TO SELECT THEATERS SEPTEMBER 2017
BECAUSE of GRÁCIA
PLAN YOUR GROUP SCREENING TODAY!
Site licensing available.
Contact info@becauseofgracia.com for more information
or visit http://www.becauseofgracia.com

BECAUSE *of* GRÁCIA

PRODUCTS AND RESOURCES

BECAUSE OF GRÁCIA: Student Guide
A Film and Faith Conversation Guide

Nine-session study guide based on three major themes of the award-winning film.

ISBN: 978-1-947297-02-9
eBook: 978-1-947297-03-6

Abbreviated leader's guides for teaching individual themes

A Film and Faith Leader Guide: Theme 1 Practicing Friendship

ISBN: 978-1-947297-06-7
eBook: 978-1-947297-07-4

BECAUSE OF GRÁCIA: Leader Guide
A Film and Faith Conversation Guide

Leader's companion to guide students through curriculum.

ISBN: 978-1-947297-04-3
eBook: 978-1-947297-05-0

A Film and Faith Leader Guide: Theme 2 Choosing Life

ISBN: 978-1-947297-08-1
eBook: 978-1-947297-09-8

A Film and Faith Leader Guide: Theme 3 Voicing Faith

ISBN: 978-1-947297-10-4
eBook: 978-1-947297-11-1

BECAUSE OF GRÁCIA: Curriculum Bundle

Includes the leader's guide, one student guide and DVD clips from the film.

ISBN: 978-1-947297-12-8

AVAILABLE WHEREVER BOOKS ARE SOLD
For ordering information, visit **dexteritycollective.co** or write to **info@dexteritycollective.co**.